DIAMONDS THROUGH WATERLOO

FALL OF THE MIGHTY

BOOK 2 in the
Diamonds through Waterloo series

LARRY FORCEY

Typesetting and cover design by Inksnatcher.

Printed in the United States of America.

Library of Congress Control Number: 2024913504

Names: Forcey, Larry, author

Title: Fall of the Mighty/Larry Forcey

Subjects: | BISAC: BIOGRAPHY & AUTOBIOGRAPHY/Baseball Biographies. BIOGRAPHY & AUTOBIOGRAPHY/Biographical Historical Fiction. RELIGION/Christian Historical Fiction.

Description: First edition. | Mesa, Arizona: Avak Publishing, 2024. | Summary: "In this second book in Larry Forcey's "Diamonds through Waterloo" series, orphan William Jennings navigates early 20th-century Manhattan and the Deadball Era of baseball, seeking answers about his past while finding solace and life lessons from baseball heroes." — Provided by publisher.

This is a work of fiction. Many of the characters are historical, and although the events described in the narrative are based on historical events, the interaction between the main characters is the product of the author's imagination. Any further resemblance to actual persons, living or dead, is entirely coincidental.

Identifiers: LCCN 2024913504 | paperback 979-8-9908961-0-9 | hardback 979-8-9908961-3-0 | e-book 979-8-9908961-1-6

Lyrics from Yellow Eyes by James Stanley Gilbert (1906) in public domain.

Scriptures are taken from the KING JAMES VERSION (KJV): KING JAMES VERSION, public domain.

The front cover photograph of John McGraw and Christy Mathewson is used by permission from the National Baseball Hall of Fame and Museum.

For information about special discounts for bulk purchases, please contact the author at larryforcey@gmail.com.

"You can learn little from victory.
You can learn everything from defeat."

Christy Mathewson

Contents

——∞——

William felt lost. Helpless. Alone.

His thoughts and daydreams had become saturated with the images of the hospital room in which Sir Thomas died.

Those final moments at his bedside were both haunting and comforting. He took solace in the words of assurance that Brother Mathias had spoken when they had left the hospital. "Brother Thomas loved you, William," he had said. "He heard your voice as you spoke, and it comforted him into the next world. You helped ease that transition."

William was not certain of the reality of that *next world* of which Brother Mathias spoke. He felt the things he had learned from the brothers at St. Mary's held value—they had taught him knowledge and skills and morals—but all the talk of God and his love and his care seemed to be more of a tale of wishes than reality.

Sir Thomas was gone. And if there was a God, the God in which Sir Thomas and the other brothers believed, how could he allow Sir Thomas to suffer as he did? How could he let him die so young? How could he allow the one person William felt closest to die?

He pondered these questions while he and Brother Mathias remained in Chicago through the weekend.

The doctor and nurses and police spoke with Brother Mathias for what seemed most of Saturday, while William spent the day with Merlin and his father, playing catch in a nearby park, waiting for the inquiries to end. When they grew tired of tossing the ball back and forth, Mr. Jones treated the boys to hot dogs, soda, and ice cream.

After William learned from Brother Mathias that they were to return to the hospital once again on Sunday morning, he asked, "Why?"

"To collect Brother Thomas's belongings," Brother Mathias answered.

"But can't we take them now?"

Brother Mathias shook his head. "The police are looking for evidence, any sign that may help them discover where he was contaminated."

William must have successfully expressed his confusion, for Brother M immediately continued. "His sickness, William. Something he ate made him sick. And there are many others who are also sick. It's important they find the source so they can try to stop others from getting the same illness."

Brother Mathias paused.

"You understand?" he asked.

William nodded. "Yes, sir."

They boarded the train early Monday morning and arrived in Baltimore in the late afternoon, just as the games on the Little Field and Big Field were coming to a close.

As Brother M held open the gate for William to enter the grounds of St. Mary's, William heard a chorus of shouting from the large expanse of grass between the two fields. He looked to his left. A large circle of boys was gathered, shouting, screaming. They were cheering on two of their classmates who danced and maneuvered with fisted hands held before their faces, each appearing to calculate the best moment to charge his opponent.

"Wait here," Brother Mathias instructed. But as Mathias rushed toward the circle of boys, William followed.

While Mathias was still yards away from the crowd, the shouting began to subside. Some of the boys who had been standing on tiptoes on the outer perimeter must have seen Brother M approaching, for one by one they began to turn, hang their heads, and step backward, making a wedge in the ring, a path that made it easy for Brother Mathias to pass unhindered into the center. And when the two pugilists saw Brother M, they each stopped their dancing and dropped their shoulders. The two boys covered their eyes with their hands, and William saw their bodies convulse from uncontrollable weeping.

Mathias wrapped his large left hand around the taller of the boys, his right hand around the other, and walked them toward the main building.

By the time William had reached the scene, the boys had scattered, faces downcast, with quiet murmurs amongst them. These skirmishes were common. The boys would be punished, banned from playing baseball, then after one or two weeks would return to the field. It seemed each child carried within him something to trigger these explosions. Each boy had his issues. And now William had another issue to add to his own collection. He looked at the scattering of boys, realizing not one of them would understand the loneliness he felt—the empty, ugly feeling that nothing at St. Mary's would ever be the same.

Who would be the new music instructor? Would he allow William to sit in the back of the classroom to listen to the music created by the other boys?

Who would read to him at night? And would they read the books Sir Thomas had read? Could he discuss the thoughts in his mind as he had with Sir Thomas?

Who would take him to next year's championship series?

"Nobody," William said softly as he stood alone on the grass field. "Nobody."

During dinner that evening, rumors of the pugilists' punishment were circulating around the dining hall. "No ball for a full month!" Congo whispered in excitement.

"They'll miss the games next week," George added. "They were two of our best."

Congo looked at nothing in particular, just staring ahead, and sighed. "We're sure to lose without them. Brother Mathias says the team from the Methodist school is one of the best in New York."

George, who normally devoured his meal and bargained with other boys to share some of their food with him, had taken two small bites of bread. He hadn't touched the potatoes, nor had he cut into the flat steak. He sat with his elbows on the table, his head rested in the cup of his hands. "A keystone and a pitcher," he said softly, "and both good hitters."

"I play keystone," William said quietly. "I pitch."

Congo and George exchanged glances as if saying, "You want to be the one to tell him?"

But William needed no explanation. He understood why neither of his two friends would consider him a possible replacement for the two pugilists. William was a year younger than Congo, two years younger than George, and he had yet to play on the Big Field with the older boys. Sure, he was one of the better players on the Little Field, but that was because he was playing with other children of his age and stature. George and Congo were special, the youngest members on St. Mary's all-star team. George was only eleven years old, and Congo was ten, but each had special skills and was tall and strong, and they could hit far and throw fast.

"Look, kid," George started.

But William held up his hand, signaling his friend to stop. "My fielding is golden," William proclaimed. "A keystone rarely needs a strong arm, so what of my lack of strength?"

Again, George and Congo exchanged glances, but this time they looked surprised. William was unsure if he had shocked them with his confidence or if perhaps he was swaying their opinion.

"And I may not have the fastest straight ball," William continued, "but my curve is the best on the Little Field. Even George can't hit it. Use me one or two innings, between the hard-throwing southpaw and the hard-throwing righty, and I'd be sure to mess up the Methodist boys' timing."

Now George and Congo were smiling. They nodded and laughed. George stood, clapped his hands, and exclaimed, "Kid, I'll protect you out there! If any of them Protestants try to mess with our keystone, I'll make sure they never do it again!"

Congo stood and wrapped his arm around George. "*We'll* make sure they never do it again!"

William welcomed this diversion. Most of the things running through his mind had to do with the fact that he would never see Sir Thomas again. He hadn't shared how he felt with anyone. Speaking with George and Congo about baseball and feigning his confidence to compete on the Big Field came surprisingly easy.

William pursed his lips. He had convinced his two friends, but that was not enough. With a demonstrative sweep of his right arm, he invited them to sit, not wanting to attract attention from the other boys. "Listen," he whispered, leaning across the table. "We need to convince Brother Mathias. Put the idea in his head. I'm glad you both like the plan, but it's his decision."

The next evening just prior to supper, Brother M entered the boys' dormitory and invited William to meet with him in Brother Herman's office. "We need to speak with you about a couple things," he announced.

Mathias had turned to leave, then quickly turned back. "And, William, bring the satchel with you."

At first, Mathias's invitation brought a surge of hope that an invitation to join the all-star team was forthcoming. But the request to bring the satchel, *Sir Thomas's* satchel, meant that more than baseball would be discussed.

Brother Herman started the meeting, expressing his sadness over the death of Brother Thomas. "If there is anything we can do, if you need someone to speak with . . ."

"Yes, sir," William answered.

Something did not feel right. On the train back from Chicago, he and Brother M hardly spoke. He and Sir Thomas did not speak much either, but that was different. It was as if they didn't need to speak. Talk was necessary only when it was necessary. But with Mathias, and now with Brother Herman, talk was a requirement.

There was something uncomfortable in the office, and all William wanted was for the meeting to end so he could join Congo and George at the supper table and eat his dinner in silence.

Brother Mathias announced that there was a temporary opening on the all-star team, and after careful consideration, they had decided that William would fill the roles of second baseman and occasional pitcher until the two boys who had been punished returned. He would pitch two innings and play second base during the game on Wednesday against the Methodist school from New York.

"Really?" William said louder than he would have liked. "Thank you, sirs. I will do my best for the team."

The two brothers cleared their throats, shuffled awkwardly toward the chairs behind them, and sat.

"We need to speak to you about something else," Brother Herman announced, pausing.

Brother M finished for him. "About Brother Thomas's briefcase."

"But Brother Mathias said I am to keep it," William pleaded.

"And so you shall," Herman answered.

"It's the papers," Mathias added. "It's what's inside that we need to see."

William unlatched the buckle and handed the bag to Brother Herman. Mathias stood and joined Herman behind his desk, sifting through the envelopes and papers. They separated the pages and envelopes into three piles. One of the stacks included staff paper on which Sir Thomas had written musical notes and measures. Another stack contained Sir Thomas's T-reports, notes on strengths and weaknesses. Some were notes on professional players, and others were about the boys at St. Mary's. And William was uncertain as to what the third stack comprised. It contained typed documents that seemed to hold importance, words and sentences that seemed to be from another language. He was grateful that he had gone through those papers the previous evening, discovering an unsealed blank white envelope that had a calling card inside. The fine print on the card read *Jennings & Jennings – Scranton, Pennsylvania.* He removed the card and placed it in a side pocket, along with some pencils.

Now Brother Herman grabbed the stack of papers, on top of which was the envelope that had held the calling card, setting it inside a drawer of his desk. If William had not discovered it and removed it, he may have never known of its existence. He hoped the two brothers would not open the side pocket, discovering the card itself.

"These notes," Brother Mathias announced, holding up Sir Thomas's reports on professional ballplayers, "we will send to Mr. Johnson."

Brother Herman handed the satchel back to William. William immediately wrapped his arms around it, hugging it against his chest. Although he had received no reprimand from Brother Herman or Brother Mathias, there was something in the way they looked at him, at each other—something that made William feel that his days at St. Mary's may be coming to an end.

***

The team from New York City was good. During fielding practice, William looked on with awe. The Methodist team had swift feet and sharp, crisp throws, indicating they would make few errors during the game. Their uniforms appeared clean and new. They were all black with the words *St. Bartholomew* written in bold red letters across the chest. Most of the players were taller than the boys of St. Mary's, and they each had a look, an expression, of confidence and certainty. The evening before when they arrived, the Methodist boys were friendly. They sat in the dining hall, dispersed among the boys of St. Mary's, and talked and laughed with one another. But now, just minutes before the game would begin, they were all business, only looking at their opponents with fixed stares of determination.

The game was scoreless into the fifth. George pitched the first four innings, striking out six hitters and giving up only two hits and two walks. There would have been three hits, but William had made a sensational play on a screaming line drive hit by St. Bartholomew's first baseman. He was the tallest member of the team and certainly looked to be the strongest. While the first baseman from the Methodist team walked to the plate to start the second inning, George stepped from the mound and directed William to take a few steps back and closer to the second base bag. William obeyed. Whereas the first three hitters of the Methodist team appeared bewildered by the pitches thrown by George, the first baseman swung at the first pitch of the second inning and hit it so hard up the middle that William ran toward the second base bag, with plans to be in position for the cutoff throw from the center fielder. But as he reached the edge of the grass that separated the infield from the outfield, he realized the ball's trajectory was only a few feet above his head. In what he initially thought would be a vain effort, he leaped as high as he could and was surprised when he felt the ball fall into the pocket of his glove. The ball was traveling so fast that William felt his mitt begin to slide from his hand, but he managed to turn his wrist enough to keep the glove from falling off, and he maintained control while he fell to the outfield grass.

Silence followed.

William supposed there was uncertainty that he still held the ball.

But when he jumped to his feet, grabbed the ball from his mitt, and threw the ball to George, who was smiling as big as William had ever seen him smile, an enormous cheer rang from all corners of the ball field. William noticed that even some of the Methodist boys stood and were applauding.

But the batter was not smiling. He was still, stopped halfway between home and first base. He placed his hands on his hips and glared at William.

"Adam," the Methodist coach shouted, "back to the bench!"

But he didn't move.

"Adam!" the coach shouted once more.

William looked at the Methodist coach, avoiding eye contact with the batter. He could tell the coach was not happy with the behavior of his player.

The coach left the dugout and approached his player. "Adam!"

Finally, the first baseman turned, shook his head, and walked back to join his team.

In the fourth inning, the Methodist first baseman hit a sharp line drive down the left field line. It was sure to be a double. But Congo, who was playing left field, rushed to the ball and made a strong throw to William, who was covering second. Instead of sliding into the bag to avoid the tag, the first baseman ran straight into William as the ball arrived, elbowing him in the torso and knocking him to the ground, the ball falling from William's mitt.

It hurt, but William would not allow anybody to know this. Not George, not Congo, not the other team, and certainly not this overgrown ape from the other team. He ran to the ball several feet away and threw it back to the mound. George looked concerned, but William paid him no heed. He ran back to his position, felt some moisture in his eyes, and waited for George to throw the next pitch.

George got out of the inning, and Mathias sent William to the mound in the fifth. William gave up two hits, but no runs. The game remained scoreless.

In the sixth, William got the first two batters out. He normally would be happy with such results but knew who was stepping to the plate next. As the first baseman walked to the batter's box, he stared at William with a cold, vengeful glare. It was frightening, but William was learning to hide his emotions. As of yet, he had spoken to nobody of what happened in Chicago with Sir Thomas. Still, he was unable to make sense of it. How could someone as kind and healthy and young and good just up and die that quick? William had written a letter to Merlin, and knowing he had someone to whom he could write seemed to help, but he was hesitant to be totally honest in the letters, afraid that he might write something that would cause his friend not to correspond.

He shook his head, hoping to chase those thoughts out of his mind. He had to focus on the Methodist ape at the plate.

George had thrown nothing but hard, straight, fast pitches to the first baseman. Actually, he threw two such pitches, and both of them were hit back into fair play just as hard. So, with calculation, knowing that his straight pitch was not even in the same speed-neighborhood as the pitches thrown by George, William aimed for the inner portion of the plate and threw as hard as he could, hoping with some certainty that the first baseman would miscalculate and pull the ball foul. As the ball left his hand, William was pleased. It was going to the exact location he hoped, sailing over the black portion of home plate.

Adam's swing was beautiful!

William admired the sound of a well-hit ball, the solid crack when the wood makes contact with the leather sphere, the wonderful sight of a sailing trajectory into a clear blue sky. And when Adam did swing, all these beautiful sounds and images occurred, making William smile at the spectacle. The ball was hit so hard, it was certain to travel off the property of St. Mary's, into the streets of the surrounding neighborhood, but it was also hit too soon. Just as William planned. The ball was foul.

Adam grunted. He hadn't even stepped from the box toward first after he hit the ball. Again he glared at William, then began to dig deep holes into the dirt.

William held the ball in his mitt, securing his fingers around the ball's seams, making sure he would throw the best curve ball of his life. The pitch started straight, traveling again toward the inner part of the plate. It was higher than his first pitch, and William smiled as he saw Adam's eyes widen while he began his swing. The ball took a quick turn downward and to the right. The bat completely missed the ball, and William rejoiced silently when he heard the ball cleanly impact George's mitt behind the plate.

"Stink!" Adam shouted.

"One more!" George yelled as he threw the ball back.

William stepped on the mound's slab and recalled how he decoded Deacon Phillippe's pitching decisions during the Series in '03. The memory saddened him for a moment, thinking of all he and Sir Thomas did that early fall in Pittsburgh and Boston.

He sighed, then looked down at his feet to make sure his foot was disclosing no secret. He wondered if the batter would be wise enough to figure something like that out.

"Not a chance," William muttered in the midst of his windup. He hurled another curve, which broke even nastier than the first. It caused Adam to take such a large swing that he lost his footing, falling on his rump in the dirt.

William skipped off the mound and trotted to the bench while the Methodist first baseman endured teasing and laughing from his teammates.

In the bottom of the ninth, the game was still tied, 0–0. William was hitless, and he walked to the plate with some shock, surprised that Brother M did not send up a more capable hitter. But after four straight pitches that were clearly over his shoulders, William recognized and admired the baseball savvy of Mathias. A small-statured batter had a greater chance of reaching safely than a good hitter against these Methodist pitchers.

The base on balls was a minor victory. William hadn't planned on making it safely to any base, but now he was trotting victoriously to first. Halfway to the bag, he looked up and saw the familiar glare from the first baseman. Only now there was a subtle smile.

William stood on the bag, desperate to hide the fear he felt. The first baseman did not speak as he approached the inner side of first base to field any pick-off attempts the pitcher may decide to throw, but instead of placing his foot on the dirt, with the side of his foot flush against the bag, the ape placed his left foot atop William's cleat, pushing down with his weight and rotating his foot, applying increasing pressure on William's right foot.

This lasted only a few seconds, but William's pain was intense. The spikes from Adam's cleat penetrated the top of his shoe and punctured his skin. He felt warm liquid begin to soak his sock.

As each successive pitch was thrown, the rhythm was the same. Adam positioned himself to field a grounder, the pitch was thrown, the batter missed the pitch, and Adam returned to cover the bag, digging his spikes into William's shoe.

Each time, the contact lasted only seconds, but the counts went full to both the leadoff hitter and the number two hitter before they struck out. William was determined not to give any satisfaction by crying out. It felt as if a pool of blood had soaked his sock, and he thought he could not endure one more episode of this pain cycle.

George was the next batter. He had hit the ball hard all three at bats but had only one single. As George stepped to the plate, William moved his foot off the bag, just before Adam's foot contacted it again. When the pitcher stepped to the mound and Adam moved into fielding position, William slammed his foot down with as much strength as he could manage onto Adam's right shoe, pushing off and running toward second, even though Brother Mathias had not given the sign for a hit-and-run.

Adam shouted in pain just as the pitched ball contacted George's bat.

William was looking toward home as he reached second, but then turned to admire the familiar high-arching trajectory of the ball, like all the other times when George had made solid contact. It was just as far and deep as the ball Adam had hit into left field, only this ball was fair and would land far beyond the right field fence since George was a true southpaw.

William sighed and looked toward first. The ape was standing with his back to home plate, staring with wonder, it seemed, at the ball George had hit.

William waited at the plate for George, with all the other boys surrounding him. When George arrived, William was the first to congratulate him and hug him. "Thank you!" he shouted, amidst the cheering of his teammates. "Thank you, George!"

George took off William's hat and rubbed the top of his head. "I promised I'd protect you, kid."

William smiled.

And when he looked one last time at the ape, his smile grew. The first baseman had plopped himself onto the first base bag, taken off his shoe, and was massaging his foot and removing his red-blotched sock.

***

As fall approached, William felt more and more alienated. George and Congo, as good friends as they had been, were permanent members on the Big Field. The excitement of the game against the Methodist school left William with an empty feeling in the games he played on the Little Field. He wouldn't attempt to explain how he felt to any of the brothers, not because he didn't think they might care, but because he didn't want to. It was as if nobody gave a second thought about the absence of Sir Thomas. And that was inexcusable.

Even though Sir Thomas was gone, William had hoped that BJ might send an invitation for that year's championship games. And if no invitation came, if Brother Mathias and Brother Herman, or any of the other brothers, would not go out of their way to take

William to the next championship, it was clear he would not be going.

Sir Thomas had died. And this was something William could do nothing about.

There would be a championship series in 1907, just as there had been in 1906 and 1905 and 1903. And if it weren't for that nasty Little Napoleon in New York, there would have been one in 1904 also. As things stood, William would not be going to the 1907 Series, but unlike the death of Sir Thomas, there was something he could do about this.

He wrote to Merlin, assuring him that he would be in Chicago for the first game. Merlin wrote back, informing William that his father had purchased tickets for the first two games in Chicago so that they could sell peanuts like the prior year. William wrote back, *I'll be there by Sunday, October 6.*

At three o'clock in the morning on Friday, October 4, William placed undergarments and socks into Sir Thomas's satchel, quietly walked down the stairs of St. Mary's, carefully opened the gate of the white picket fence, and walked two miles to the station, where he waited for the westbound train to Chicago. He dressed in the best clothes he had, just as when he had traveled with Sir Thomas. He sold all his candy and gum to the other boys over the past several months, sensing that at some point he would need to have cash to do what he was about to do.

At 6:30, he followed a large family toward the conductor checking tickets. He figured his presence alone would require explanation, fearing he'd be forced to return to St. Mary's when he was discovered. So he huddled close to the last children in the large family as they ascended the stairs into the train. He handed his ticket to the conductor, sat in a seat next to a window, and waved good-bye to Baltimore, wondering if the boys and the brothers would miss him as little as they seemed to miss Sir Thomas.

The next two days were a blur. Everything seemed to work perfectly. He arrived in Chicago without any complications. Only once did someone on the train ask about his family, and he answered honestly that he was traveling to see his friend—his family could not come, so he was traveling alone. He feared this may lead to further inquiries, but none came, and when he was welcomed by Merlin and his parents at the station in Chicago, he nodded at the woman who had inquired about his family. The woman walked by, ignoring William, and went out of her way to change direction as if to avoid him and those welcoming him to the Windy City.

The following day was game one. The ceremonies and pomp of opening another championship series caused William to anticipate equal excitement on the field, but none came. The game was dull until the late innings.

The Cubs had held a 1–0 lead since the fourth, until the Tigers scored three in the top of the eighth. But the first two hitters in the bottom of the ninth reached safely and scored, tying the game at three. In the bottom of the eleventh, with one out and the bases loaded, Johnny Kling, the Cubs catcher, was standing on third, Johnny Evers was at second, and Schulte was at first. William looked on, with certainty that the Cubs were about to take a 1–0 Series lead against the American League champion, Detroit Tigers.

Billy Donovan had pitched the whole game for Detroit, and from William's perspective he was still as strong as when the game started.

"Ain't no way he gettin' outta this," Merlin shouted above the cheering crowd. "We got it in the bag!"

William looked over at his friend and nodded. He looked behind him, then to his left and right. The entire crowd was on its feet, applauding, shouting even louder perhaps than when the Cubs tied the score two innings earlier.

Joe Tinker, the slick-fielding shortstop, was next in the batting order, but Frank Chance, the Cubs manager, sent Heinie Zimmerman to pinch-hit. It didn't work. Zimmerman struck out. The bases remained loaded. Two outs.

Having used his entire bench, Chance had nobody left to pinch-hit for Cubs pitcher Ed Reulbach, who grounded out to the shortstop, ending the inning.

William sighed. He looked at Merlin, whose shoulders sagged, and he lowered his head, shaking it side to side. The entire crowd fell silent. And the sky was darkening.

The Tigers were retired one-two-three in the top of the twelfth. In the bottom of the inning, with one out, Sheckard was hit by a pitch, bringing Chance to the plate.

Immediately after Frank Chance was thrown out at first, completing an inning-ending double play, the home plate umpire, Hank O'Day, removed his mask and pointed to the sky. He moved his hands across one another, as if calling a baserunner safe, then with a broad sweep of his right arm, shouted, "Game is called. It's a tie."

Although O'Day did not officiate the prior year's Series, William recognized him from the first two Series. Sir Thomas had explained that O'Day had been one of the better pitchers during the early years of professional ball and later became an umpire. He was likely the most respected of all the officials, even though he was not well liked. With little sense of humor and a serious businesslike demeanor, he had a short fuse for antics and arguments. "Look at his pants," William recalled Sir Thomas telling him, "how nicely pressed they are! His tie, perfectly in place!"

Since O'Day was calling the game, there would be little argument from either side. His word was final.

William looked at the sky, as did most of the fans. The sky was more black than blue.

Within a few minutes, the West Side Grounds had transformed from a loud, raucous circus into a somber procession of twenty-four thousand baseball fans filing out into the streets of Chicago.

"At least we sold all the peanuts!" Merlin smiled, patting William on the back. "We'll get them tomorrow!"

William had other concerns. There were rumors that the games in Detroit were sold out. Bennett Park only had a little over eight thousand seats, creating a black market for ticket sales. What were normally one- or two-dollar seats were being sold for over ten dollars. How was William to attend? And what havoc was the tie game going to cause? What was to be the best of seven was now going to be the best of eight.

Merlin's father had promised William some money for his work. "Young Mr. Jennings," he had said, "I will pay you 20 percent of your sales."

William had counted his money prior to the start of the game. He had sold out of peanuts, with the cash in his pockets totaling $23.25. "That's over $4.60," William muttered, before Orval Overall had thrown the first pitch of the game to the Tigers leadoff hitter, Davy Jones. If sales were this good tomorrow, that would be over nine dollars. Now, walking to the train station, William realized that there would be three games, not two, in Chicago. And this revelation made him smile. Perhaps, he thought, he would have enough for at least one game in Detroit.

Jack Pfiester held the Tigers to one run in game two as the Cubs scored three off the Tigers' George Mullin. Pfiester held Detroit's top two hitters, Sam Crawford and the young phenom Tyrus Cobb, to one hit in eight plate appearances. William was greatly disappointed with Cobb. He had read over the past year of the great hitting prowess of this young hitter from Georgia, but in two games he had only one hit in nine at bats.

In game three the Cubs' pitching again kept the Tigers' offense quiet. Crawford and Cobb each had one hit, hardly enough to keep up with the Cubs. The final was 5–1, and the Cubs players could enjoy the eight-hour train ride to Detroit, knowing they held a 2–0 Series lead.

"Don't take this the wrong way," Merlin told William as they stood on the platform at Union Station, waiting for the train William would board for Detroit, "but I'm hoping we don't see one another till next year."

William understood Merlin's sentiment. They had discussed it numerous times, most recently the previous evening as they lay on the two mattresses in Merlin's bedroom, speaking of their plans if the Series returned to Chicago. If it didn't, William's plan was to travel east to New York City.

But he would need to find a way to survive. He had read enough books and glanced at enough of the newspaper pages surrounding the sports scores to know that the textile industry in Manhattan was enormous. Because of the skills he had learned at St. Mary's, he figured he should have little difficulty finding a shop that would hire him. Sure, he had read Jacob Riis's *How the Other Half Lives*, had thumbed through the pictures. He knew of the plight of child laborers and the dangers and oppression of those who worked in the textile industry. Sir Thomas had spoken of this a couple times, and though William felt some horror at what he heard from Sir Thomas, he was curious and excited about experiencing the things of which he had only read.

William smiled as he thought of a witty response to Merlin's comment. "And what makes you think the Cubbies will win the National League again next year?"

"Ducky," Merlin started. "I declare! Are you just teasing? You were there. With Overall, Reulbach, Pfiester, and Three Finger Brown, and that lineup, their stolen base antics and great defense, ain't no team able to keep them from next year's pennant."

Merlin was right. William nodded, thinking of the lesson Sir Thomas had taught him of great players and great teams: they learn from their mistakes, their failures. The Cubs had lost the previous year to their hapless crosstown rivals. The White Sox were renowned for their great pitching and horrendous hitting, yet the Cubbies' offense proved even more hapless than their opponents the previous year.

Whatever they had learned from that loss was helping them silence Detroit.

"We'll see," William answered, as the train whistled in the distance.

William turned and smiled at Merlin's parents standing a few yards away. He walked to them and hugged them. "Thank you, Mr. Jones. Thank you, Mrs. Jones."

"Unlike my son," Merlin's father said to William, "I am hoping to see you in a few days. We could use a few more games."

Mr. Jones did not get his wish. The Tigers fell to the Cubs at the first game in Bennett Park by the score of 6–1. The Cubs held a 3–0 Series lead and had yet to use their best pitcher, Mordecai Brown, who was scheduled to pitch the next day. The sequence of events was a great benefit for William. Although he did have to pay eight dollars for a standing room ticket for game four, the tickets for the next game were being sold for less than face value since most of the fans in Detroit had given up hope. For one dollar, William purchased a ticket for a seat behind home plate to watch Three Finger Brown shut out the Tigers, 2–0.

Although Cobb had been a disappointment, getting only four hits in twenty at bats, William felt some pride in witnessing the Cubs overcome their humiliation from the prior year to gain the Series victory.

———∞———

He sewed and ironed and pressed and cleaned.

Within hours of arriving from Detroit, William was working in a shirt factory on Canal Street.

He had boarded the train fearing that perhaps it was best to return to Chicago and live with Merlin and his parents. They had offered, but the lure of New York was too great. Merlin's home was warm, it was clean and fun, and William felt safe there, but he had also felt safe within the walls of St. Mary's. What he wanted more than safety and more than a home was something he couldn't describe. But he felt that in Manhattan he might find it.

William imagined he had been magically transported into one of the pictures he had seen in that book on Sir Thomas's shelf, *How the Other Half Lives*. William recalled the horror Riis captured— the plight of textile workers, including children—seeing it as if it were occurring far away in another country. Now he was seeing it for himself. Adults of all ages working alongside children, sweat saturating their tattered clothing as they tailored fine shirts and pants and dresses that sold for more than the weekly salary of the workers. The stench in the factory was unbearable, but William hardly noticed it after the third day. At St. Mary's he had worked alongside George and Congo for three hours each afternoon. Now he tailored for ten hours, six days a week. The adults received ten dollars as they left the factory each Saturday evening. The children received six. William might have thought of complaining, but he heard reports that other factories paid children much less. There was one mill that paid anybody under the age of sixteen only three dollars for a sixty-hour workweek. William observed that managers did not tolerate those who spoke without being spoken to, so he worked and kept silent. Each week when he received his six dollars, he'd fold it neatly in half and place it in his pocket, and after finding a solitary location outside, being certain that nobody was watching, he'd remove his left shoe and place the money in the envelope he kept there. When the envelope got too thick, he divided the cash equally between his shoes.

But there was a panic in 1907 that created a dubious outlook on paper currency, so the managers began to pay in coins. William spent the coins when necessary but traded his unused coins for paper since it was easier to store. When the envelopes grew too thick for him to walk comfortably, he reluctantly began to place the cash in the inner pocket of the satchel and guarded it with even greater protection than before since its value now was both sentimental and financial.

Twelve weeks had passed since he arrived, and he had earned seventy-two dollars. Twenty dollars were in the envelope he kept securely in his shoes and forty had been transferred to the satchel. He had eventually found a place to stay that cost him only five cents each night. It was within walking distance from the textile district, two blocks east and five blocks north, at 327 Rivington Street. He had learned of it from the older children with whom he worked. When he arrived in mid-October, the weather was still warm enough to sleep comfortably in a park or under the steps of a church, but when the weather cooled in early November, his first plan was to find a room at the nearby Henry Street Settlement home. But when he learned that these apartments were occupied by families and that nurses employed by the settlement lived in the units on the top floor, he feared that his circumstances might lead to someone reporting him to the police and his being sent back to St. Mary's, or worse, somewhere else. So, he remained on the streets as long as he could and, desperate to find a warm place to sleep, entered through the doors at 327 Rivington in mid-November.

A wooden sign was nailed above the doorway. The bold gold letters, outlined in black, read "Children's Aid Society – Rivington Street Home." Although it was after eight o'clock, the halls were scattered with children walking or running through hallways and up the staircase. William watched a young boy jump from one stair to the next, holding a towel in one hand and a toothbrush in the other. William turned, looking in all directions. He saw no dust, no dirt, no footprints on the floors, and noticed no foul smell in the air. Electric lights illumined the hall. He breathed deeply, closed his eyes, and smiled, hoping that he would be able to call this place home.

And it was his home for the next two months until his circumstances at the factory turned sour. The wealthy man whose business paid its child workers three dollars per week had purchased the factory where William worked. After William received his first three dollars, he decided to not return. He figured it would be easy to find similar work for more pay. And it was. The following day he began sewing buttons on shirts at a workshop on the corner of Grand and Essex. He left after two weeks, mostly because the conditions were so horrid. He could have endured the weekly wage of five dollars, but he feared catching some disease from fellow workers who coughed deeply and without ceasing. He found another job on Canal Street but did not return the next day for similar reasons. For two weeks he searched and found work but did not stay long enough at any job to get paid.

It was mid-April, and William figured he deserved a day off. Until now, Sundays were the only day he was free to explore the city. The two things he wanted most to do were to visit the three ballparks and the many libraries throughout the city. But the libraries were closed on Sunday, and the city's blue laws prohibited ball games from being played on Sunday.

On Friday, April 17, William woke at five in the morning along with the other children at the Rivington Home, and strapped the satchel around his shoulder, but instead of turning left onto Rivington toward the garment district, he turned right and walked north about one mile, then turned left on Tenth Street. He was told by the night watchman at Rivington that after two blocks, the library would be on the right side of the street, directly across from Tompkins Square Park.

The directions were perfect. He arrived at the library a few minutes after seven, almost three hours before it would open. He walked across the street, removed the satchel from his shoulder, and sat on a wooden bench on the north end of the park. He raised the satchel and pressed it against his chest, squeezing it tightly, and fell asleep.

When he opened his eyes, he reached into his right pants pocket for the watch that had belonged to Sir Thomas. He clicked open the lid and felt relief when he discovered it was 9:30. He smiled, not so much because he hadn't missed the opening of the library, but because he felt a strange feeling of freshness. He figured it was a benefit of the nap from which he had just awakened, but he never recalled such a feeling from the many required naps he had taken during his days at St. Mary's. He rose from the bench, strapped on the satchel, and raised his arms to the sky, letting out a yawning sigh that increased the growing peace he felt inside.

He looked to his left and right, considering what he might do to occupy the next thirty minutes, when he noticed a church a couple blocks to the north. He squinted, trying to read the name of the church on a wooden sign pounded into the lawn outside the sanctuary: St. Bartholomew's Methodist Church.

Curious, William crossed Tenth Street and walked north on Avenue B toward the church. Could it be, William thought, that the team he, George, Congo, and the others had beat in the fall of '06 attended this church?

He walked up the steps and considered knocking on the sanctuary doors but figured nobody would be in a sanctuary on a Friday morning. He searched for any sign that this was the same St. Bartholomew's as the baseball team that visited St. Mary's. There was a picture in a glass-encased bulletin board to the right of the doors. William shuffled over to examine it. The photo showed a middle-aged man standing next to a pretty woman. Below the picture were all sorts of announcements on various sizes of paper. On one of these pages, written in large, thick black letters, the title read *Child Employment Placement.* Beneath the bold letters, William read:

> Washburn Manufacturing is offering safe,
> clean work environment for children in need
> of earning wage for their family. Pay begins at
> $7.00 per week, Monday—Friday, 8 a.m.—6
> p.m. Interested applicants can report to Mr.
> Washburn's office at the corner of Twelfth
> Street and Avenue C.

William let the satchel slide from his shoulder. He bent to his knees and reached inside, searching for a pencil and paper. He wrote the address from the announcement, folded the paper into quarters, and placed it in his vest pocket.

He opened the watch again. The library would open in five minutes. He strapped the satchel back over his shoulder and skipped to the front doors of the library.

He had a lead for a job with better pay and an extra day off per week. He had over a hundred dollars in his shoes and satchel, and he had the rest of the morning to spend in the library before going to Hilltop Park to watch the Highlanders play the visiting Athletics. This was developing into a great day.

He walked through the front doors of the library and examined the layout. Except for the middle-aged lady behind the desk near the right-hand wall, he was the only person inside. He wasn't sure what to do first. There were so many shelves in so many aisles with so many books of so many sizes. Next to the lady at the front desk was a stack of three newspapers. William approached her and cautiously reached out to touch the top copy.

"May I?" William asked, his eyes dancing from the librarian to the paper.

"Certainly, dear," she answered. "Just place it back here when you are finished."

William smiled, grabbed the paper, walked to a table just behind him, and sat. He placed his satchel on top of the table and began to turn the pages of the newspaper until he found the listing of baseball scores.

The Giants had lost the second game of the season to the Phillies, 3–6. Their record was 1–1. He had hoped to watch them play at the Polo Grounds, but they were in Philadelphia.

The Highlanders, on the other hand, were hosting Philadelphia's American League team just a few blocks east of the Giants home park. Although William would have preferred to see the Giants, the opportunity to watch Connie Mack's Athletics would suffice. He opened the satchel and removed the sheets of paper on which he kept notes on key Giants players—Joe McGinnity, Christy Mathewson, Art Devlin, Fred Tenney, Roger Bresnahan.

He found the page of notes focusing on the Giants losing pitcher, Red Ames, from the previous day. He scribbled some notes, folded the newspaper as nicely as he could manage, then walked back and placed it with reverence as close to the location as he could recall in front of the librarian.

"Young man," she said, "I've not seen you before."

"No, ma'am," William answered. "I live further south, near Rivington Street."

"Do you have a library card?"

William shook his head. "No, ma'am."

She reached under her desk and handed him a sheet of paper. "You complete this form, and you can borrow any book you like."

"Any book?" William repeated.

The librarian smiled. "Just as long as you promise to return it."

"Yes, ma'am."

As he was completing the form, from the corner of his eye he noticed something on the carpet. It was the card he had taken from the white envelope a year earlier, just before he left St. Mary's. It must have fallen from the side pocket when he swung the satchel off his shoulder. He'd need to be more careful.

He reached down, picked it up, and set it before him, next to the application for the library card.

"Jennings and Jennings. Scranton, Pennsylvania," he whispered, looking up toward the librarian.

He wondered whether something in all these books might help him find an address, a way for him to contact this Jennings & Jennings to ask whether they might be any relation to him.

He finished the application and handed it to the librarian.

"William John Jennings," she announced as she wrote his name on a small card, "you are hereby invited to borrow any book from the shelves of the Tompkins Square Library. As often as you like."

"Thank you, ma'am." William reached up for the card and placed it in his vest pocket, then stepped up closer to the librarian's desk, holding up the Jennings & Jennings card. "Do you think it may be possible . . . I mean to say . . . whether we could find out who this may be? Where exactly in Scranton they are located?"

The librarian reached down and held the card close to her eyeglasses, then moved the card away and lowered her head, her eyes peering over the top of her glasses.

"Relatives of yours?"

William shrugged his shoulders. "Maybe."

"I'll see what I can find." She smiled and handed the card back to William.

He exited the library, turned right on Tenth Street, and walked to the closest elevated train stop that would take him to Hilltop Park.

He arrived one hour before the game, paid twenty-five cents for his seat, and watched the players from the Athletics and the Highlanders stretch and play catch and interact with fans. Five minutes after the first pitch was thrown, he was bored.

William looked from the first baseman to the second baseman to third and shortstop, from left field to center and right, from catcher to pitcher. Not one of them, except perhaps the Highlanders right fielder, gave William hope that he would witness excitement on the ballfield. When the Athletics took the field in the bottom of the first, his despondency heightened. Sure, Jack Coombs was on the mound for Philadelphia, but he was no Chief Bender or Eddie Plank.

In the second inning he looked out toward the Highlanders right fielder, Wee Willie Keeler. How he would have liked to see him play when he was younger. Sir Thomas had told him the stories of Keeler and McGraw, how they changed the way the game was played, making it more exciting for the fans. Yet, Keeler was no longer the brilliant hitter or lightning-fast runner he once was. Now he was shuffling his feet through the thick outfield grass, struggling to keep his batting average around the .250 mark. For fifteen straight years he had eclipsed .300, once hitting .424, "the very year you were born," Sir Thomas had once told William. "Why," Sir Thomas had continued, "you were likely born during his forty-four-game hitting streak!"

William sighed and pouted and hunched his shoulders. It was now the third inning. He looked at the scoreboard, just behind the standing crowd on the outfield grass. In bold white letters across the top was written *American League*. Underneath the first three innings, the scoreboard operator had hung six large green metal plates, each with a bold white *0* painted on it. Three had been hung to the right of *Philadelphia*, and three had been hung to the right of *New York*.

"Boring," William muttered.

But even closer to the crowd, just to the right of the American League scoreboard, was a smaller scoreboard on which New York's National League game was displayed. As updates from Philadelphia were received by telegraph and news spread to the men in charge of the numbered plates, the New York fans could follow the progress of their city's more exciting team.

It was more difficult to see since many of the fans standing on the outfield grass prevented William from having a clear view. When a *3* was hung next to *New York* on the National League scoreboard under the third inning, William straightened in his seat and imagined how the Giants scored their runs.

In the fourth inning the Athletics scored the first runs at Hilltop Park, scoring three in the top of the inning. But William hardly noticed. His attention was focused on the National League scoreboard. He was becoming anxious, wondering what might be taking the scoreboard operator so long in hanging up the plates for the fourth inning. Could it be, William thought, that the Giants were having a big inning? When the operator finally hung up the plate, it displayed only a *1*.

Minutes later he hung up another plate, under the fifth inning. On it was painted a *5*. Under the seventh inning a *2* was hung, under the eighth a *1*, and under the ninth, *2*.

"Fourteen runs!" William rose from his seat, applauding with other fans as each new number was placed next to *New York* on the National League scoreboard. The Highlanders had been defeated by the Athletics, but nobody at Hilltop Park seemed to mind. The loudest cheers of the day followed the placement of numbered plates on the National League scoreboard.

The next morning he ran to the library to study the box score. He placed the newspaper next to sheets of paper he had prepared the night before, each with the name of one of the Giants players written at the top. Art Devlin had a single, a double, and a triple, but no other player had more than two hits, and although the team had scored fourteen runs, the Giants players had only earned eight RBIs. And only the light-hitting shortstop, Al Bridwell, had more than one. And he only had two.

William looked up from the paper. He scratched his head and studied the game once more. He had anticipated more offensive exploits than what appeared in the line score. The pieces of paper on which he had written the names of the Giants players with such enthusiasm seemed pointless. He was hoping for doubles and triples and maybe one or two home runs. But the greatest accomplishments were a triple, three doubles, and a bunch of singles.

He looked at the names of the Phillies pitchers in the game. The starter, Lew Moren, had given up the first nine runs. The next pitcher, Harry Coveleski, gave up two runs, and the third pitcher, Buster Brown, surrendered the final three. William realized that of the three pitchers, Coveleski fared the best, yet a story beneath the game summary reported that Coveleski had been sent to the Phillies minor league team after the game. Moren had surrendered nine runs in just over four innings, Brown had given up three runs in two innings, and Coveleski had given up two runs in two and two-thirds. If Coveleski did better than the other two, why was he the one demoted?

As William searched the newspaper's narrative for more information about the unfortunate Phillies pitcher, he reached to his right where he had strewn the pieces of paper with Giants players' names, grabbed his pen, and drew a line through *Art Devlin*. In its place he wrote the name *Harry Coveleski*.

He scribbled the details of his performance from the prior day: *2.2 IP, 3 Hits, 2 Runs, 1 ER, 1 BB, 1 K*. He drew the large *T* that Sir Thomas had taught him to make and on the left side of the page wrote *SENT TO MINORS*.

William eyed the right side of the *T*.

"Mr. Coveleski," William whispered to the sheet of paper, conscious that he was in a library, "what will you do now?"

***

The following Monday, William reported to Washburn Manufacturing. Within minutes of his arrival, they placed him on the floor that tailored shirts. After a week of work, when he received his first seven dollars on Friday evening, he decided he would remain there, he hoped for a long while. He learned that the Children's Aid Society hosted another home for child laborers a few blocks from his new workplace, and soon he received permission to relocate.

His new home and his new workplace were both within a mile of Tompkins Square Library. Each Saturday he spent the morning hours gathering information from the newspaper and compiling notes, creating a notebook of T-reports. He asked the librarian to hold copies of all the weekday editions, and she did. Each Saturday when William walked to her desk, she smiled and handed them to him.

Maybe she was going out of her way because she felt badly for finding no information about William's inquiry in Scranton. This saddened William initially, but there were other libraries in the city with other librarians that may have better resources.

On Monday, June 8, when William arrived at the factory, the other children were waiting outside the warehouse, sitting in chairs that had been arranged in a semicircle around a wooden stand that reminded William of one of the music stands in Sir Thomas's classroom.

"We have a new manager," one of the older boys whispered.

All the boys, it had seemed to William, were happy with the man who had been their supervisor. What had happened to him? William swallowed nervously as he glanced from one coworker to another.

The side door from the main building opened. The owner of the company was the first to emerge and walk toward the boys. William had met him during his first week at the company, and each time he encountered him since that day, Mr. Washburn had addressed him by name. "William Jennings, how are you today?" he would say, as they passed each other in the hall or arrived at work in the morning. He was a tall man who wore a nice, clean, pressed suit with a vest and tie. His shoes seemed to sparkle.

Standing a few feet behind Mr. Washburn was a tall young man, not much older than William and the other boys, dressed in almost identical manner. And his shoes sparkled.

"Boys," Mr. Washburn began, "I would like to introduce you to your new supervisor."

William did not need the introduction. He recognized the young man immediately—the first baseman from the St. Bartholomew's baseball team.

"This is my eldest son, Adam." Mr. Washburn announced.

For the first two weeks, as each day passed, the initial anxiety William felt subsided. He made extra efforts to avoid his new manager and conscientiously focused his attention on one of the other boys or on the shirt he was tailoring in order to avoid their eyes meeting. He began to wonder whether perhaps Adam did not recognize him and feared what might happen if he did.

The other boys spoke well of their new supervisor, and from William's perspective, the quality of all their work improved. It dawned on William during late June that he had seen most of his coworkers at some point in conversation with Adam, but as of yet, the two of them had not spoken.

Each morning, Adam walked behind the boys as they were sewing and made comments, usually positive, about the quality of their work. Never had he made any comment to William.

On the first day of July, during his daily observation of the boys' work, Adam stopped directly behind the chair in which William was seated. The usual ease and routine with which William sewed buttons on a collar left him. His right hand was trembling, and the more he tried to control the trembling, the more he trembled. The needle he held pricked his left index finger, and blood dripped onto the white cotton shirt.

"Follow me," he heard Adam say, as though he had been rehearsing for the moment.

William rose from his seat and followed his supervisor to a desk in the far corner of the warehouse.

Adam waited for William to sit in the wooden chair on the outside corner of the desk, then sat in an upholstered chair behind the desk. He opened the desk's drawer and reached inside. "Here," he said to William, his hand holding a bandage. "This will help stop the bleeding."

William reached out, wrapped the bandage around his finger, and cautiously said, "Thank you."

"The work you do is very fine, Mr. Jenkins," Adam stated.

William looked up. "It's Jennings," he corrected, and he immediately regretted saying it.

"Is it?"

William nodded, but with little certainty.

"For all we know," Adam continued, "you may be a Buhler, or a Mansinni, or a Sousa, or a Sadinsky, or whatever. Yes?"

William felt his heart race. He squinted and shrugged his shoulders and looked to the floor.

"Listen. These other boys may look up to you. My father says you do the finest work of the bunch. But neither the boys nor my father knows who you really are. Only you and I know. Am I right?"

William looked up. Was he to speak an answer or just remain silent?

"You do what I tell you, and all will continue as it has since I arrived. You keep doing your work. You keep getting your seven dollars each week. Who knows? Maybe even more if you impress me."

These words frightened William. Adam was smiling. He was tapping the eraser head of a pencil on the wooden desk, and this only increased the anxiety William felt.

"You have two options here, Jenkins," Adam pressed on. "You agree, or I send a telegram to Baltimore."

William again looked to the floor and found courage to look Adam in the eyes.

"What would you have me do?" he asked.

Adam rose from his seat and extended his hand toward William. "Trust me," he said.

William looked behind at the other boys in the distance. All of them were busy with their work. How he envied the routine.

"All you have to do is trust me," Adam said once more, his hand still extended.

William stood, cautiously shook Adam's hand, and walked back to his seat.

Five minutes prior to closing that evening, Adam approached one of the boys that worked at the table next to William.

"Jenkins!" Adam shouted. "Over here, please."

William laid the shirt onto the table before him, softly caressed it as he pushed himself out of his chair, and approached Adam and the other boy.

"Yes?" William asked softly.

"Charles here has stolen from the company. Buttons have disappeared from his box."

William turned to look at Charles. He hadn't known the boy's name. He didn't seem to be the stealing sort.

Adam continued. "Of course, he denies it, but you know differently. Yes?"

William pointed his finger into his chest. "Me? But how—"

But Adam interrupted before William could continue. "In the office earlier today, we spoke of it."

William turned to look at the boys at his table. The comradery he had come to recognize and appreciate was gone. Each of the boys wore an expression of suspicion, anger, distrust.

Across the warehouse, all the boys looked at William with similar glares.

He had to act quick. He would not acknowledge any truth in Adam's accusation. And if he disagreed with him, he'd be relinquishing any cards he held.

He would need to take action—and decide his own fate.

He stepped toe-to-toe to Adam and looked up.

His brain was full of words he wanted to speak, but he feared his emotion may interfere with the message he hoped to convey.

"Listen," he started. "You are a horrible supervisor."

Oohs and *aahs* echoed throughout the floor. William felt he had landed a punch, so he continued.

"You manage as poorly as Napoleon managed at Waterloo."

Silence surrounded them. William was on a roll. So he continued.

"He could have won if he were not stubborn and full of his narcissistic obsession of victory, setting his generals up for failure and blaming them for his downfall."

Adam's eyes appeared to have reddened. But what William had interpreted as a preface of anger instead evolved into a sinister grin.

Adam raised his head and scanned the floor. William turned to look at the boys, who seemed to be in a stupor, uncertain how they ought to respond to the events unfolding before them.

When he turned back around to face Adam, his supervisor's grin evolved into a smile, then laughter.

William heard a faint giggle from a boy in the far corner of the factory. Then another, followed by more, until a chorus of laughter filled the warehouse.

William hung his head.

He turned and raced outside.

That evening he checked out of the Boys' Home, and with only his satchel and $200, he walked toward the west side of the city, hoping to find work and shelter in one of the Newsboys Homes run by the Children's Aid Society.

***

The next morning, after finding a room but not a job assignment, he decided to explore the libraries on the west side of the city. The librarian at Tompkins had been helpful in securing the weekly newspapers for him to study, but she was of no use in William's growing desire to explore who he was, from where he came. Being raised at St. Mary's was all the evidence he needed to confirm that he was what society referred to as an orphan. His parents did not want him.

He felt that the card in Sir Thomas's satchel might lead him to family, especially since his name appeared twice on the card: *Jennings & Jennings.*

But as nice as the librarian was and as willing as she had been to assist William, there were no books or newspapers, no documents of any sort at the Tompkins branch that proved helpful.

He found numerous directories at the St. Agnes Library on Amsterdam Avenue between Eighty-First and Eighty-Second, but the information was limited to local residents and businesses.

The librarian at St. Agnes directed him to another library several blocks north, also on Amsterdam Avenue, just before One Hundredth Street. When he reached Ninety-Fifth Street, he saw a large gray stone structure rising high above the surrounding buildings. Four sets of Greek-like columns held up a façade on which dignitaries had been sculpted. William looked up and imagined the awe he'd currently be sharing with Sir Thomas if he were only by his side. It reminded him of the Jewish church they both admired, where they had met Sir Thomas's rabbi friend three years earlier. He had recognized the synagogue one evening as he was walking home. Once he became familiar with the streets on the East Side, he'd walk past it each morning and evening, reminiscing of the adventures he had shared with Sir Thomas and wondering if he would approve of the choice William made to leave St. Mary's, or if he would be proud of how he had found work and a safe place to live on his own.

Two boys rushed past, waking him from daydreams. As they ran up the steps, William noticed the large sign that confirmed he had found the Bloomingdale Library.

Discouraged by the little progress he was making in finding an address for Jenning & Jennings, he found some solace in discovering the many libraries of the city. He imagined New York as a world map, each library its own nation. In the "eastern hemisphere" was the Aguilar Library on 174th, representing Russia. Further south, on Ninety-Sixth was one of the libraries funded by Carnegie, its central location leading William to surname it the "Austro-Hungarian library." His home library, Tompkins, depicted Europe, and Chatham Square on East Broadway stood for Australia. In the "western hemisphere" were the Cullen Library on West 136th, the location equivalent to Canada, and the Bloomingdale on One Hundredth, representing the United States.

As he reached to pull open the large wooden entrance door, he noticed the two boys who had rushed by him seconds earlier now cursing at one another while the older-appearing boy attempted to mount a bicycle that clearly belonged to someone much taller. The boy on the bike was instructing his friend to do something with the seat as he placed his feet on the pedals. Unable to do anything about the seat's height, the boy on the bike brushed the other boy aside, placed his feet on the left pedal, and pushed down. But the pedal did not move. Instead, the boy lost his balance and tumbled to the concrete, the bike falling on top of him.

William looked behind. Nobody else was on the library steps. Nobody had entered or left the library since William arrived. Still holding the door with his left hand, he opened it enough to look inside, wondering if he should report the actions of the boys to anyone.

But he saw only two people inside the library: a woman working behind a desk, her glasses and hair almost in identical arrangement as that of the Tompkins Square librarian, and a tall, slender man dressed in a grayish flannel suit.

William looked back at the two boys. They were arguing and pushing one another, the older-looking boy still holding the bike, examining it.

He looked at the man in the suit, whose height was certainly sufficient for William to conclude that the bike the boys were trying to abscond with belonged to him.

William rushed inside. "Sir," he whispered. "Sir, is that your bike outside?"

The man did not turn around. He had just pulled a book from a shelf and was reading it when William stepped closer.

"Psst," William said a bit more loudly. "Hey, is that your bike outside?"

Still the man did not turn, his only movement the turning of pages.

William looked across at the librarian and, as best he could, quickly examined the rest of the library to see if there were other people who might be upset if he spoke a little louder.

"Mister!" William said, in an attempt to be louder than a whisper but softer than a shout. "You own a bike?"

Nothing. The man turned another page.

William looked across again at the librarian. Their eyes met, and she shrugged.

With caution, William crept to about two feet from the man and lightly tugged his coattail.

The man turned and smiled at William.

It wasn't the man's broad shoulders or his smile that affected William most, and it wasn't the slightly cleaved upper lip or his clean-shaven face or his hair parted down the middle, making him appear younger than William assumed him to be, but it was something about his eyes, something that communicated to William a kindly frustration that he recalled seeing frequently on Timmy's face.

Instinctively, William raised his hands and signed, "Is that your bike outside?"

The man's smile grew wider. "Yes!" he signed back.

William had grown confident in his ability to communicate with Timmy, but he had never attempted to communicate with an adult who was hearing impaired. He swallowed nervously and tried to communicate as well as his limited vocabulary would permit. "Two boys are . . . well, I think they are trying to steal it."

William would not have thought it possible, but the man's smile broadened even more, and his laugh echoed through the aisles of the library. It was a deep, bellowing laugh, snarled and awkward. William looked around, but only the librarian was in the vicinity, and she appeared amused.

The man cupped his hand over his mouth—William guessed he was aware of the noise he must have just created—then tapped

William on the shoulder, and with mischief in his eyes, signed to William, "Follow me."

The man raced to a side exit door of the library and held it open for William. Once they had both stepped outside, the man raced to the corner of the building and peered toward the library's front entrance.

The boys had made some progress. They had managed to carry the bike down the stairs of the library, but their attempts to pedal were useless. The other boy was trying now. At one point he stood on both pedals, and while his friend held the handlebars, he jumped off the bike seat several inches into the air and landed back on the pedals. Still, neither pedal budged.

The awkward laugh William had heard in the library again burst forth from the man. He began clapping his hands and placed his hand over his eyes, wiping tears that had slowly began to trickle down his face.

It took a while for the man to compose himself. He removed a handkerchief from his vest pocket, then walked toward the two boys. He looked back at William and waved with his hand for him to follow.

"You'll talk to them for me—yes?" the man signed to William.

William nodded.

Another attempt of the two would-be thieves ended with one boy on the ground, the handlebars bruising his chin.

The man reached down and helped the boy stand.

"This is your bike?" the man signed toward the boys.

The two friends looked at one another uncomfortably, surprised maybe, but certainly, William surmised, they had no idea what to do next.

William called out to them. "He wants to know if that is your bike."

Again, the boys looked at one another, then turned and sprinted toward the west entrance of Central Park.

Although the laughter of the man was not as boisterous, he was still clearly amused as he inspected his bike.

"Not bad," he signed to William. "Just a few scratches and nicks."

"You can ride it then?" William signed. "They didn't break it?"

The man waved William closer. "Come here," he invited. "You know a C-clamp?"

"C-clamp?" William signed back.

"C-clamp," the man repeated. "We use them on the farm. Come here. Look here."

The man bent toward the rear wheel and unscrewed a small device attached to the wheel's rim, braced and tightened against a portion of the bike's frame, near enough and tight enough that it kept the wheel from turning despite the force the boys had placed on the pedals.

Next, the man took a tool from his pocket and did something to the pole that held the bike's seat in place. When he was finished, the bike seat was much lower than it had previously been.

"Now," the man turned and signed to William, "you sit. You ride."

"But . . ." William struggled to figure out what he should sign, not because he did not know the correct signings, but because he had never ridden a bike, and though he wanted to learn, was not sure he wanted to embarrass himself in front of this man he was beginning to admire.

"First time?" the man signed. "Very good. I will show you. I'll stand next to you, and we'll go in the park. It's much safer than the street."

By the time they had reached the end of the park at 110th Street, William was able to ride without his new friend's assistance. By the time they reached 130th, William began to wonder how much further he was to travel. He didn't mind, since the next library he planned to visit was on 168th Street, just a few blocks past the Polo Grounds.

"I work up this way," the man signed to William. "You can ride to my work."

When they passed 150th Street and 155th, then 156th and 157th, William's heart began to race. He saw just in front of him the large rock formation from which fans could watch ball games for free.

"This is it," his friend signed, as they arrived at a large wooden building just beyond the large center field expanse of the Polo Grounds.

William swung his feet off the frame of the bike and walked with reverence toward the chain link fence that served as security for the Giants ballplayers.

He turned quickly, raised his hands, and signed, "I'm such a dummy! You're Luther Taylor!"

His friend laughed, placed his right hand atop William's thick hair, and rubbed it several seconds. William had read that ballplayers liked to do this for good luck—find a young fan on the way to that day's ball game and run their hands through his hair.

Luther bent to his knees and looked William in the eyes. He signed slowly, using letters, not words. "My close friends call me L-U."

William nodded, but he did not feel worthy to assume such familiarity with one of the Giants most beloved players. He fumbled with his fingers and hands, scrambling to find the signs to express his thoughts. "Why, just two days ago, you shut out the Robins in Brooklyn."

Luther smiled and nodded.

"McGraw ought to let you pitch more." William grew more confident with each word he signed. "You'd have more than five wins if he only let you pitch more days."

"Step inside," Luther invited, "and you can tell him yourself."

William wasn't sure if his new friend was serious. He had already sensed that Luther enjoyed a good joke, and he wasn't sure if the invitation was genuine.

"Do you have plans today?" Luther continued.

"No," William answered.

"Would you like to shag some fly balls for the boys?"

William turned his index finger toward himself and poked it into his chest. "Me?"

Luther set the bike against the fence and stood facing William. He bent slightly to his left as though he were trying to make sure he had William's attention. He raised his right hand and pointed to the same general spot on William's chest that William had just poked himself. At the same time, he clearly mouthed the word, "You!" as though he were shouting it, and a noise did protrude from Luther's lips, though it did not sound like any word William understood.

"Yes, you," Luther continued signing. "And who shall I be introducing to Mr. McGraw when we see him on the field?"

"William," he signed. "My name is William Jennings."

***

Thursday, July 2, 1908, was the most magical day William recalled—certainly the best day since Sir Thomas had departed. And some of the feelings he had had during that first game they attended in Boston, watching the Pirates win the first game of the first World Series, stormed into his memory as he watched the game from the row just behind the Giants dugout. Toeing the slab just about sixty feet away was Christy Mathewson.

Matty had won the first six games he pitched that season and currently had a 13–5 record, with six shutouts. It was all in the notes inside William's satchel.

Each year Matty's prowess on the mound increased. After watching Matty pitch three shutouts against the Athletics in the '05 World Series, Sir Thomas had handed a sheet of paper to William on the night they returned to St. Mary's. Just before he began that evening's bedside reading, he handed the piece of paper to William and said, "I want you to study this." On the top of the page was Matty's name. The large *T* that Sir Thomas used to record his player evaluations was directly below his name, and on the left side of the paper Sir Thomas had written Matty's pitching statistics from his first season with the Giants in 1900: *Zero Wins, 3 Losses, 5.09 ERA, 33.2 Innings Pitched, 37 Hits, 20 BB, 15 K.* "What happened?" William recalled Sir Thomas asking. "What happened between 1900 and 1901? What changed?"

William never could figure it out completely, but something had clicked for Matty during the off-season or during the early part of the 1901 season. He was still walking a lot of batters, but the number of hits he surrendered per inning decreased considerably. He won twenty games in 1901, fourteen in '02, thirty in '03, and thirty-three in '04, the year McGraw refused to play in the World

Series. Then in 1905, he won another thirty-one. The numbers were incredible, and although his performance seemed to be on the decline in 1906 and 1907, winning only twenty-two and twenty-four games respectively, 1908 was looking to be his best year yet. And William had a front-row seat.

Manager McGraw approached William after the game while the rest of the team and coaches walked across the outfield grass toward the clubhouse in deep center field.

"William Jennings?" he said, walking up to the railing, in front of the seat where William sat. "Luther tells me you can play ball."

William felt frozen.

This was a man he despised. The man responsible for canceling the Series in '04. The man he pictured as a devil, someone who embodied all the bad of Napoleon and none of the good.

Not confident he could speak intelligibly, William resorted to nodding his head.

"Here," McGraw said, tossing a mitt toward William.

William caught the mitt and slipped his left hand into the worn leather. It was a much higher-quality glove than he had ever placed on his hand.

McGraw lightly tossed a ball toward William and waved him onto the field.

William caught it, hopped over the railing, ran several feet from the Giants skipper, turned, and tossed it back toward McGraw.

McGraw caught the ball without having to move the mitt. He took two steps back and threw the ball, with a bit more juice, back toward William.

William caught it, threw it back. On target again.

McGraw took another two steps back and threw with more speed.

This cycle continued for about five minutes. William was standing a few feet behind home plate and a bit on the first base side of the field, and McGraw was a few yards on the outfield grass, somewhere between first and second base.

"Can you be here tomorrow?" McGraw shouted, as he threw the ball back to William.

William reached to catch the ball, and it fell snugly in the pocket.

McGraw motioned for William to join him on the outfield grass.

"Twelve o'clock," McGraw announced. "Each home game. Three dollars per game. You can take one or two balls home each afternoon, do with them what you like. You'll clean our uniforms. You'll clean our shoes. You'll keep the clubhouse clean, and you'll keep the dugout in order during the game. Bats in place, always side by side, never crossing one another. Players don't like that. Superstition. Understand?"

"Yes, sir."

"You may receive tips from the players. That is fine. They will ask you to run errands. Players are a funny bunch. If they ever ask you to do something you don't feel comfortable doing, come to me. Understand?"

"Yes, sir."

McGraw placed his hand on William's shoulder and patted it softly several times. "Very good."

For a man whom he had previously disdained and feared, he began to feel that Little Napoleon was an appropriate nickname.

***

Although Mathewson was having the best season of his career, the Giants were struggling. For most of the year, they had been stuck in third place, unable to gain ground in the standings on Pittsburgh and Chicago. In early August they finally caught up to Pittsburgh and managed to stay in second place behind the Cubs for about two weeks. Then on a road trip out West visiting St. Louis, Cincinnati, and Pittsburgh, they won nine straight, overtaking the Cubs.

A few days later the Cubs swept them, creating a tight race as the two teams entered the final month of the season.

William had done his job well. He cleaned and kept all in order, just as McGraw instructed. He had settled into another job as a newsboy, which allowed him to earn more money than he had been earning at Washburn Manufacturing. He used his extra cash to buy a selection of vests, coats, and hats with which he dressed strategically each morning, depending on the news on the front page of the paper. If there was a business merger or the federal government was causing grief for one of the monopolies, he would grab a vest and tie and fedora that gave him the appearance of a miniature Wall Street executive. He'd station himself outside the elevated train exit closest to Wall Street and shout out the day's headline. If the story regarded a visiting dignitary, he'd go to the government district, but if there was a visiting symphony, he'd station himself near the art district. If a new display was arriving at the museum, he'd go to the stop closest to the museum.

He was paying five cents each week for a place to sleep. And the Newsboys Homes had something the other Children's Aid Homes did not have: bank account boxes provided by one of the local Manhattan banks, giving the boys a place to safely store their cash. William's five-hundred-dollar savings was no longer kept in his shoes.

The Giants had another bat boy who traveled with the team to the visiting cities. William got along with this older boy but envied him for the opportunity to travel. After each home game, William would rush to the Washington Heights Library and compile notes on the events at the Polo Grounds. The following morning after he had sold his newspapers, he would purchase one paper for himself and spot-check his notes with the write-up of the game in the *New York Times*. When the Giants went on the road, William relied on the newspaper accounts solely.

On September 1 Matty pitched his tenth shutout of the season. His record had improved to twenty-eight wins and eight losses. The Cubs were only half a game back, but the Giants kept surging.

William had been writing letters to Merlin, bragging about the Giants' ascension to the top of the standings. Merlin would write back, reminding William that the Cubs would not give up the fight and had won the last two National League pennants.

On Friday, the 4th of September, the Giants were playing Philadelphia, and the Cubs were in Pittsburgh. As was his custom on Saturday morning, William kept one of his morning papers and went to the Bloomingdale Library. He read about a strange occurrence during the game between the Cubs and Pirates. With a scoreless tie after nine innings, the Pirates player-manager, Fred Clarke, led off the bottom of the tenth with a single. Tommy Leach sacrificed him to second. Honus Wagner hit a sharp grounder up the middle that was knocked down by Johnny Evers, preventing Clarke from scoring. William leaned forward, lost in the narrative. The next batter, Warren Gill, was hit by a pitch, and the bases were loaded. The second baseman, Eddie Abbaticchio, struck out, leaving it up to the Pirates right fielder, John "Chief" Wilson, to win the game. He lined a clean single into center field to score the winning run. But the drama began after Clarke had crossed the plate.

The newspaper account detailed how the Cubs second baseman, Johnny Evers, began shouting at Jimmy Slagle, his teammate in center field, to throw the ball to him at second. Once Evers got the ball, he touched second base and immediately began yelling to the umpire, "Hey, O'Day," trying to get his attention. But Hank O'Day had already turned his back on the field and was walking to the clubhouse. Evers finally caught up to him, and with his manager, Frank Chance, explained to O'Day that the Pirates runner on first base, Gill, had never touched second base following the clean single by Chief Wilson. Since this constituted a force-out, they argued, the run scored by Clarke should not count and the game should remain tied at zero.

O'Day agreed with the interpretation of the rules, but he confessed that he was not paying attention to whether Gill had reached second base safely. Since he was the only umpire on the field, he could not confirm whether Gill had touched the bag, and he could not make a ruling. The newspaper hinted that O'Day was sympathetic to the Cubs' predicament and offered that if it were ever to happen again, he'd be ready to make the right call.

A little less than three weeks later, on Wednesday, September 23, at the Polo Grounds, the Giants and Cubs were tied 1–1 in the bottom of the ninth.

At the Washington Heights Library, William wrote a letter to Merlin an hour after the game ended. He raced to the post office to place the letter in the mail, hoping that his firsthand account would clarify the chaos Merlin was sure to read about in the Chicago papers the following morning.

September 23, 1908

Dear Merlin,

Remember that game the Cubs lost to Pittsburgh a couple weeks ago? We thought O'Day was just blowing wind, trying to make the Cubs less upset, since he didn't know what else to say about their protest? Well, it happened again!

By this time you've read the facts of the game. And I am guessing you are left confused. Well, I was there, and I am confused.

I am sure you were aware that our two teams had the exact same record before the start of the game and that Pittsburgh trailed us both by just a game. All this clutter at the top of the standings, and only a handful of games left to play to decide who would win the league pennant. And then this happened!

It makes it all the more chaotic!

The game was scoreless after four. The Giants had two hits against Pfiester, and the Cubbies had two against Matty. Then your light-hitting shortstop, Mr. Tinker, hit a home run in the top of the fifth, thanks to a muff by Devlin in right. In the bottom of the sixth, Herzog scored the tying run. And it remained tied at one until the bottom of the ninth.

Seymour started the inning by hitting a weak grounder to Evers. One out.

Art Devlin smashed a Pfiester fastball for a single. McCormick hit a hard grounder to Evers, who of course gobbled it up quick and threw it to Tinker to beat out Devlin at second. Two outs.

Our promising young first baseman, Fred Merkle, sliced a hard liner into right field, just over the outstretched reach of your manager, Mr. Chance, but it was hit so hard Merkle could only make it to first base, and McCormick was standing on third.

Then it was the turn for our light-hitting shortstop to take center stage. On the first pitch from Pfiester, a pitch so low that O'Day would have surely called it a ball, Bridwell smashed a clean single up the middle—hit so hard that the infield umpire, Bob Emslie, lost his footing as he danced to get out of the way, did a somersault, and fell on his rump. This is an important fact to remember: Emslie was preoccupied, his attention drawn away from the events transpiring on the field. For as he was raising himself from the ground, his back toward home plate, just as McCormick scored the "winning" run and McGraw, who had been coaching at third base, was following in his wake, dancing like a crazed leprechaun, the craziness began.

Fans had already jumped from the stands to congratulate the team. Since the clubhouse is way out in center field, Matty, McGinnity, and all the other veterans on the team knew that in order to emerge from the circus on the field after a walk-off hit, they must sprint toward center field before they got intercepted by the frantic crowd. And this is a message they teach the younger players. Earlier in the year, Merkle was caught in the mass of fans on the Polo Grounds infield, unable to join the team in their clubhouse celebration.

What I found odd was that Joe McGinnity had not rushed to center field, as was his custom. Neither was he celebrating with the fans on the field. He had been in the first base coaching box when McCormick scored the winning run, but I saw him scowling as he walked toward your second baseman, Mr. Evers.

Evers was waving his hands at Solly Hofman in center, begging him to throw the ball. All that was transpiring before my eyes had a scary resemblance to the report I had read about the game the Cubs lost in Pittsburgh on September 4.

I looked toward home plate, and there was Hank O'Day. He had removed his mask, holding it in his right hand while he focused his attention on Evers and Hofman.

Hofman threw the ball to Evers, but it was off target and bounced several yards away. That's when McGinnity ran to pick up the ball. His intention was clear: he was about to wind up and throw the ball as far as he could into the crowd in the right field bleachers, but Evers wrapped his arms around McGinnity and climbed onto his back, trying to wrestle the ball out of McG's grip. But McG is much larger than Evers, and it didn't take him long to shake free. Then he threw the ball high and far. And it disappeared into the unsuspecting crowd.

While all this was going on, the crowd captured Matty, set him on top of their shoulders, and carried him toward the clubhouse. I turned my attention back to Evers. He found another ball, from where I do not know, but it was not possible for it to be the ball McG threw away seconds earlier. This ball Evers held high, making sure he had Hank O'Day's attention, pounded it into his mitt, and stomped his right foot onto the second base bag.

Neither umpire responded to Evers's gestures, which seemed to create even more fire in his antics. He began yelling at O'Day, pointing his finger, waving his hands, shouting at Emslie.

After several seconds of this, I noticed O'Day slowly nod his head, tilting it side to side, as if he was remembering the promise he made Evers and the Cubs back in Pittsburgh couple weeks earlier.

He raised his right arm and with his fist signaled that the runner at second base was out. Fred Merkle had not touched second base (and I can tell you this is a fact—I saw him race toward the clubhouse, assisted by Matty before Matty was intercepted by the throng of fans). He had made it maybe as far as halfway between first and second but never touched the second base bag.

I am sure the Giants will protest O'Day's decision.

If the league decides it's a tie, they will have to play it again later.

But not much later. There are only fifteen games left in the season!

Say hello to your parents for me.

Your friend,

Ducky

The following day, William sold his papers and rushed to a small café in Washington Heights, two blocks from the Polo Grounds. He had wanted to read the accounts of the game, but there was such a high demand for the newspapers that he had no time. Men rushing to work handed him a nickel, then continued on their journey while they flipped the pages of the paper, paying more attention to the paper than their physical surroundings. William assumed they were doing what he would like to do—turn to the summary from yesterday's game and read the comments from the local sportswriters.

But now, all alone in the café two hours before he needed to report to the clubhouse, William ordered a hot chocolate and a slice of bread and read the following editorial in the New York Times:

> Censurable stupidity on the part of player Merkle in yesterday's game at the Polo Grounds between the Giants and the Chicagos placed the New York team's chances of winning the pennant in jeopardy. His unusual conduct in the final inning of a great game perhaps deprived New York of a victory that would have been unquestionable had he not committed a breach in baseball play that resulted in Umpire O'Day declaring the game a tie.

"Merkle's boner," the fans were calling it on the streets. William reached into his satchel and pulled out an unused sheet of paper. He wrote *Fred Merkle* on the top of the page, then with two quick strokes of his pen drew the *T*.

Merkle had shown such promise as a young hitter. William had been certain he would be a star. He wrote *Merkle's boner* on the left side of the *T* and wondered if anything good would ever be written on the right-hand side, if Merkle would be able to emerge from the mistake he had made.

The Giants beat Mordecai Brown and the Cubs that afternoon, Matty relieving Wiltse in the seventh, one day after his nine-inning start.

When William arrived home that evening, before going to bed, he searched for the T-report he kept for Brown. It was already several pages long. He wrote an *L* next to the date, *Thursday, September 24*, then updated Brown's record to *25–9*. He searched for Matty's report and wrote a *W* next to the date, updating his record to *34–9*.

As much as he liked Matty, and as proud as he was to see him daily at the Polo Grounds and to hear Matty call him "Mr. William," unlike most of the other players who would call out, "Boy," he revered Three Finger Brown. Brown's report was his favorite. Of all the T-reports, William kept only those players that had proven their worth in the satchel—who had risen above the ashes of failure and shined on the diamond—and of all those, Mordecai Brown was his favorite.

The very first line on the very first page described in two brief sentences the corn shucker accident that Brown suffered when he was seven years old, resulting in the loss of most of his index finger and middle finger. It provided the most beautiful example of the reporting technique which Sir Thomas had taught William: a bad thing written on the left-hand side of the *T*, which for Brown was the loss of two fingers, and on the right side of the *T*, the blessing that loss created, allowing Brown to throw the most devastating curve in either league. Some said it was even more difficult to hit than Matty's fadeaway pitch. Matty's T-report, on the other hand, had hardly any failures or struggles listed, only the poor showing in his rookie season. It was easy to understand Matty's success. He was tall, handsome, well educated, and was raised by a loving father and mother. He had all the tools for success. Brown, on the other hand, rose from tragedy.

***

Two days after the tie game, the Giants fell into second place. Within a week, President Pulliam announced his agreement with O'Day's ruling, and the game was a tie. If necessary, it would be played again.

There had been so many games canceled earlier in the year because of bad weather that almost each day during the final two weeks of the season, the Giants played a doubleheader. On Friday, the 25th, they lost two to Cincinnati. Then on Saturday they won two from the Reds.

Then the Phillies arrived.

On Monday the Giants beat them, 7–6. On Tuesday they won the first game of a doubleheader, 6–2. The second game was to be pitched by the young Philly hurler, Harry Coveleski, who had been sent to the minors back in April.

William knelt on the steps at the corner of the Giants dugout, mesmerized, imagining what thoughts were dancing through the mind of Coveleski. Would he again be hit hard by the Giants? Was this the final opportunity the Philadelphia organization would give him? Or would he, like Matty back in 1901, find some way to turn his career around?

Coveleski hit a leadoff triple in the top of the sixth, starting a five-run rally. He gave up seven hits to the Giants, struck out six, and allowed nobody to score. The Phillies won, 7–0. The Giants again fell into second.

"He didn't have that," McGraw muttered in the dugout, late in the game. Nobody seemed to hear him, as though he were talking to himself. It was a normal occurrence during a game. Players just seemed to assume that he was strategizing, thinking out loud, so only when he made eye contact would a player venture to say, "Did you say something?"

McGraw was looking up and down the dugout, but all the players seemed lost in their thoughts, perhaps wondering why they were unable to rally against a pitcher they hit so well just several months earlier.

"That's new," McGraw said, this time focusing his eyes on William. "That curve. It's new! It's beautiful! We didn't see it in April!"

William nodded.

"Son of a—" William heard McGraw shout, then stop short as if he cared a child was within earshot of his comments. He never seemed to care previously. Little Napoleon shook his head, bit his lip, then continued his rant at a much lower volume, almost at a whisper, yet its volume rising with each epithet that spewed from his mouth. "That scum-suckin' . . . boot-lickin' . . . scab-chewin' . . . ," stopping short again, looking at William square in the eyes, and, nodding, with a tone of respect for the Phillies' hurler, "That muckrackin' Polack learned a new pitch!"

McGraw's praise for Coveleski reminded William of Napoleon Bonaparte's words spoken to the fallen Russian officer at the Battle of Austerlitz. He dared not smile at the good feeling this gave him, fearful of making McGraw upset, but at the Washington Heights Library after the game, he found in his satchel the sheet he created for Harry Coveleski. He had thumbed through his library of reports at the Newsboys Home that morning, knowing Coveleski would be on the mound for the Phils and hoping he may do something that would earn him a home amongst William's favorites in the satchel. He looked up to the library's ceiling, wondering what words would best describe what occurred at the Polo Grounds that afternoon. He placed the pencil on the paper and wrote, *The new curve may salvage his career.*

Three days later in Philadelphia, Coveleski beat the Giants again, 6–2. Two days later he outpitched Matty, winning 3–2. After this loss the Giants fell to third place, behind both Chicago and Pittsburgh. He had defeated McGraw's team three times within a week. The New York sportswriters tagged Coveleski with the honored nickname, the *Giant Killer.*

It was Monday, October 5, with three games left in the season, and the Giants' only hope was to sweep the visiting Boston Braves. The Pirates had already lost a makeup game to the Cubs on the 4th of October, ending their season with a 98–56 record. The Cubs' record stood at 98–55, and they would win the pennant if the Giants lost any of their three remaining games to Boston.

The Giants swept the Braves, outscoring them 19–4 in the three games. They ended the season with a record of 98–55, identical to the Cubs. The tie game would have to be replayed to determine who would win the National League pennant.

The Giants players were bitter. McGraw was livid. "I don't care whether you fellows play this game or not," he told them in the clubhouse after they had swept the Braves. "It's up to you all. As far as I'm concerned, you are the champs of the National League."

That evening a group of players led by Matty visited their ailing owner, John Brush, to discuss what they ought to do. William waited outside the hotel in which Brush was staying, hoping that his services would be needed the following afternoon. "We're on," Matty said as he met William outside the hotel. "The Grounds will be crazy tomorrow," he warned. "You best arrive early."

William skipped to the Newsboys Home, as he was sure all the people he passed on the streets shared his anxious excitement. He envisioned a raucous atmosphere, similar to what he and Sir Thomas had witnessed in Boston back in '03.

***

October 7, 1908

Dear Merlin,

It's Wednesday night. Big makeup game tomorrow. Too excited to write. Won't get much sleep. I promise to write more after game.

May see you before you get this letter. If the Cubbies win, I am going to quit selling papers and get on the first westbound train to Chicago.

October 8 – Thursday

I woke at four.

The sun still hadn't risen when I reached Central Park. Still, I could see a large crowd gathered at one of the nicer hotels on the west wide, blowing horns, ringing cowbells, shouting and singing and banging drums. I walked over and discovered it was where your Cubbies were staying. I can't imagine they got much rest. I'm sure that was the intent of the fans.

I arrived at the Polo Grounds just after six and went straight to the clubhouse. I had to maneuver around to make sure not to step on the thousand or more fans who slept outside the ticket windows.

The smudgy windows and the wobbly stools and rusty nails that the players hang their hats and uniforms doesn't seem right. These are the New York Giants! I swept the floor and tried to make the clubhouse look extra clean. I scrubbed grass stains off Devlin's jersey. I took a rag and rubbed the dirt stains from off the pants of Herzog, Bresnahan, Donlin, and Seymour. I stood facing Matty's stool, reached out and touched his uniform, bowed my head, and pleaded, "Let his straight ball travel fast. Let his curve ball break far. Let his fadeaway fall from the face of the earth."

By eight o'clock I was done. The floors sparkled, the uniforms were clean, the cleats were cleared of dried mud and grass. I walked outside and the crowd in the streets had grown. The line at the ticket windows now extended two blocks more. I felt I needed to escape. I took a train south and spent a couple hours on the north end of Central Park. As I was eating on a park bench, I spotted Bill Klem, the Homeplate umpire scheduled for the game. Then I recognized the Giants team doctor, Dr. Creamer, walking up to him. Fast like. In a hurry.

The doctor tried to hand an envelope to Klem. Money? But Klem shoved him in the chest, turned, and walked away. Later, on my back to the stadium, I saw Klem again, this time with Jimmy Johnstone, the other umpire for the game. Fans began to yell at them and some even pushed them away from the Polo Grounds. Maybe I could have tried to help, but what could an eleven-year-old kid do?

The game wasn't supposed to start until three, but somehow McGraw got the league to change the start to 2:30. As the Cubs arrived, I began to understand why McGraw wanted the earlier time. The Giants were having infield practice when the Cubs tried to take the field. When your manager, Mr. Chance, refused to go back to his dugout, McGinnity pushed him from home plate, pointed to the visiting dugout, raised a bat and waved it at Chance's head. Both teams rushed to their teammate. The umpires hadn't arrived yet so each team did their best to control Chance and McGinnity. It took a while for tempers to cool, then both teams made their way to their dugouts – still screaming and pointing at one another.

A bit later I heard shouts and yells from the outfield area where fans were packed behind ropes. The chain link fence in right field had fallen and the police were using a fire hose to spray the crowd with water.

It got worse!

Beyond the rightfield bleachers, I saw a man climb one of those poles that hold up the train tracks. Probably wanted to watch the game for free like those who sit on the large rock behind home plate. But the man fell and people screamed when he must have hit the ground. Not long after, I saw two men on the top of the right field bleachers pushing one another. One of the men lost his balance and fell onto the field. I learned later that the man falling from the pole had died and the man falling from the bleachers broke his leg.

One last thing I should tell you before the game begins. I was on the outside of the dugout, near Bresnahan as he warmed-up Matty on the sidelines. They both looked worried. The pop I usually heard when Matty throws was gone. It was more like a thud. And when Bresnahan signaled for Matty to throw his curve, there was little arch, certainly not enough to fool the Cubs.

When Sheckard struck out to start the game, I looked at Matty. Then looked at Bresnahan. Neither looked surprised. But when Matty took a deep breath and shook his head before making his first pitch to Evers, I felt he was not just shaking off the signal Bresnahan had given for the next pitch, but was shaking his head in wonder that he had started the game by striking out your leadoff man with a fastball that was not fast and a curve ball that did not curve. Evers grounded out to Herzog, and then Matty struck out Schulte. Bresnahan pumped his fist in his mitt on the third strike, and Matty walked like he always does from the mound – like a warrior victorious in battle. I felt my heart pounding in my chest, wondering how in the world did the Cubs not hit the junk Matty had thrown.

Pfiester hit Tenney in the left arm with his first pitch. Did Dr. Creamer offer money to Pfiester also?

Chance was not happy. He stood at first with his hand on hips. The look in his eyes reminded me of the look one of the brothers gave us when we misbehaved in class. I wondered how long he would leave him out there. Pfiester walked Bucky Herzog next, then struck out Bresnahan. He picked off Herzog at first, but then Donlin hit a hard double, scoring Tenney. Next, he walked Seymour. We were up 1–0, two men on. And if Herzog didn't get picked-off, Pfiester would really be in a mess!

I looked at Matty. Matty was looking at Merkle at the far corner of the dugout, all by himself. He had asked McGraw not to play him. I kid not, Merlin, this guy had been eaten alive by the writers and fans. Every time he stepped to the plate, a bunch of boos and hisses would rise in volume. He looked horrible—sick like. Gaunt. He's lost at least twenty pounds since that September 24th game.

Anyhow, back to the bottom of the first. When I saw Matty look at Merkle on the far end of the dugout, I looked at Merkle and saw him smiling—something I would never have imagined possible. But that smile was gone pretty quick when Chance left first base, walked toward Pfiester, grumbling, then shouting "I've seen enough!"

Chance motioned to the sideline and soon Three Finger Brown came jogging to the mound.

Once Brown finished his warm-up pitches, I looked at Matty. I looked at Merkle. I looked at everyone on the bench, and even McGraw. Some were biting their lips, scratching their heads. None were smiling.

Brown struck out Devlin to end the first.

Matty continued his magic act in the second, striking out two more Cubbies.

Brown made quick work of us in the bottom of the second, retiring McCormick, Bridwell, and Matty on less than ten pitches.

Then came the top of the third.

Tinker stepped to the plate. Matty turned and waved at Seymour out in center, motioning him to play deeper. Seymour either didn't see Matty or disagreed. Tinker hit it sharp, on a line, right at Seymour. He took one step in, and that was it. The ball sailed over his head, and by the time he caught up to it and threw it back to Bridwell, Tinker was standing at third. Kling hit a clean single, scoring Tinker and tying the game. Brown bunted Kling to second, and Sheckard hit a lazy pop to Herzog for the second out. Matty walked Evers intentionally (Matty fears Evers more than any hitter, even more than Mr. Wagner). Schulte doubled. Chance doubled. By the time Steinfeldt struck out to end the top of the inning, your Cubbies were up, 4–1.

We got two singles in the bottom of the inning but left Tenney standing on third. Then one-two-three, one-two-three, one-two-three—that was the rhythm of the fourth, fifth, and sixth innings. Brown was making quick work of us.

Finally, in the bottom of the seventh, Devlin led off with a single, only because Tinker slipped and fell after fielding the ball. Then McCormick singled and Bridwell walked. The bases were load for Matty, nobody out. That's when McGraw signaled for Smiling Larry Doyle to hit for Matty. As I passed Matty to hand Doyle his bat, I saw a fire in his eyes. I didn't hear him say anything to Little Napoleon (I have learned that they are good friends, their wives do everything together, and they even live in the same apartment building). So I wasn't surprised when Matty said no angry words.

Doyle hit a foul pop behind the plate, and my heart sank. Kling camped under to make the catch even as a soda bottle sailed past his face, thrown by an angry fan. Tenney hit a fly ball to right that was deep enough to score McCormick, but then Herzog hit a routine grounder to Tinker to end the inning. We had bases loaded, no outs against Brown, and only managed one run. We were down 4–2 with six outs left. I heard Merkle repeating over and over and over to whomever would listen in the dugout, "It's all my fault, boys. It's all my fault, all my fault." But nobody said anything to him. The crowd was silent. No cheers, no horns, no cowbells.

Brown continued the one-two-three rhythm in the eighth and ninth. It took him all of four pitches to get the last three Giants out.

The game was over.

If we had won, the fans would have jumped onto the field and raced to the players. They would pat them on the back and lift them on their shoulders. But now it was like a funeral.

Most of the players had left the field and begun moping. As I cleaned both dugouts, I saw isolated skirmishes on the field. Some Giant fans were trying to interact with the Cubs players, maybe trying to start fights. It got so bad that the police removed their revolvers and held them high like they were ready to use them. The police gathered your team and led them to streetcars waiting outside.

When I arrived in our clubhouse, most of the players were still in uniform. They sat on their stools or on the floor. They sat with their backs against the lockers. They looked at the ground. They shuffled their feet. They didn't speak.

Merkle was in McGraw's office. I could hear him saying, "Get rid of me. Fire me. I've blown it for all of you . . ." But McGraw responded quick and loud, saying stuff like, "Fire you? Why, you're the kind of guy I've been lookin' for for so many years. I could use a carload of you. Forget the season and come back next spring. The papers will have forgotten it all by then."

Just when I think he's the meanest guy on the field, he says stuff like this.

Matty was the last to leave. He had just stayed on his stool, staring at the concrete floor. Finally, he picked up his bag and walked with head down toward the exit. Since my work was done, I followed him out toward Eighth Avenue. That's when I heard applauding and shouting and cowbells and horns. A couple seconds later I stood just behind him, looking out at the hundreds of fans. "I did the best I could," Matty told them. He raised his head and turned it to the left and right. "But I guess fate was against me." He raised his right hand and waved at the crowd, looked back at me, and laid his hand softly on my shoulder. And nodded with a forced grin.

"Thanks for being here with me, Mr. Jennings," he whispered.

And that was it.

I went to library. Wrote this letter. I will drop it in the mail. And walk home.

I will see you before you get this letter. And we'll watch your Cubbies spank the Tigers for the second year in a row.

Your friend,

Ducky

***

The Series between the Cubs and Tigers was anticlimactic, a bore. Even Merlin did not appear enthused. William had hoped to see the Tigers score more runs than they had during the previous World Series. In the five games played against the Cubs in 1907, the Tigers had scored a total of six runs—and three of those were in the first game, which ended as a tie. Cobb had done little to impress. Even Sam Crawford had been held in check by the Chicago pitchers. But of even greater disappointment was the absence of the antics displayed by Detroit's manager, Hughie Jennings.

William had learned of Jennings's prowess as a player from listening to Little Napoleon speak of him to the Giants in the dugout or on the field during batting practice. The two, William concluded, had been good friends and teammates when they were younger. Just his name sparked William's curiosity. "Jennings," William thought when he first heard McGraw speak his name. "How many Jennings are there in the world? And am I related to any of them?"

Detroit's manager had habits on the ball field that entertained the fans. The habits' frequency and awkwardness had direct correlation with the success of the Tigers' offensive exploits. Since Detroit struggled the previous year against the Cubs, William did not recall witnessing any strange occurrences in the third base coaching box from which Jennings managed. But in the bottom of the seventh of the first game, with the Cubs up 5–1, Cobb led the inning with a single, Rossman singled, Downs doubled, and the pitcher singled, scoring three and getting the Tigers within one run. The next inning, the Tigers scored another two to take the lead, 6–5. Once Cobb had scored in the seventh and Rossman was racing around third to score the second run of the inning, the

Tigers manager jumped high, landed on his right leg while keeping the left leg bent and dangling in the air, raised his arms over his head, and in a high-pitched scream, shouted, "Ee-yah!"

With each successive run the Tigers scored, the "ee-yah" grew louder. He shouted "ee-yah!" for as many times as there were total runs scored. So when the Tigers scored their sixth run in the bottom of the eighth, the redheaded manager repeated the jump and shouted, "Ee-yah! Ee-yah! Ee-yah! Ee-yah! Ee-yah! Ee-yah!"

He chattered constantly with the Cubs third baseman, but Steinfeldt did not make eye contact with Jennings and showed no signs of being bothered. If there were no men on base, Jennings cupped his hands over his mouth, creating a makeshift megaphone, and shouted obscenities that sounded very similar to the words William regularly heard McGraw shout at the Polo Grounds.

The Tigers manager's bright red hair and fair skin differed greatly from William's dark hair and olive complexion, so there was little chance they were related. But was there a Jennings out there, somewhere in America, whom he may call family? Would visiting Scranton in search of Jennings & Jennings help discover any truths about his past?

The Cubs scored five runs in the top of the ninth, dashing the Detroit fans' enthusiasm to win a World Series game. William boarded the train for Chicago, sold peanuts with Merlin outside of Westside Park, and watched the Cubs defeat the Tigers, 6–1.

In the third game, Detroit finally won, scoring five runs in one inning and besting the Cubs, 8–3. The next two games were in Detroit. The Cubs shut out the Tigers in game four, and the Cubs shut out the Tigers in game five. The Cubs were the first to win consecutive World Series, and the Tigers were the first to lose consecutive World Series.

William would not return to Chicago. He would not return to New York. At least, not yet.

In Detroit he boarded the southbound train, traveling through Cleveland and on through Pittsburgh.

At the station he wrote detailed notes while the lady at the ticket window dictated train numbers and cities in which to disembark, describing how he might navigate to Scranton.

1909

He awoke to a deep, bellowing, repetitive echo of *oompa, oompa.*

With a sweep of his left arm, he pulled himself from under the covers and dashed to open the hotel window. Now he heard the other rhythms, other instruments in unison with the tuba: the rolling of a snare drum, the melody from a clarinet, the racing keys of an accordion. He pulled the window further up and stretched as far as his body allowed, searching. To his left just a block away, he saw a band surrounded by a group of men and women who were dancing, circling one another. The men, dressed in lederhosen, twirled the women, who were dressed in thick green skirts. Crowds lined the streets, clapping and singing to the band's melody.

William felt himself smiling. His foot was keeping rhythm. He looked down at his right foot, amused that the longer he listened, the higher and more excited his rhythm-keeping became.

There was no time to brush his teeth or wash his face. He rushed to the closet, put on his knickers, vest, and hat, grabbed his jacket, slid his shoes onto his feet, and raced down the stairs.

He had been here six years earlier with Sir Thomas, and hearing the band play filled him with those good memories. The Pirates had played Boston back in '03, and now they would be playing Detroit.

After the Series ended the previous year, he had journeyed to Scranton. Whether the instructions he received were faulty or the notes he had taken were erroneous, he had gotten lost and somehow found himself in Shamokin. It hadn't been catastrophic, for the following day he was able to catch another train to Scranton, and in hindsight, it was an advantageous diversion. A festival similar to the one he was now enjoying had been taking place in the park near the center of town. A local Shamokin band was playing, including tuba, clarinet, accordion, violin, and drum. And William recognized the drummer.

At first he doubted it could be him, but the conversations he heard between the two men he sat behind at the park confirmed his suspicion: the drummer was Harry Coveleski, the Philadelphia Phillies pitcher whom New York sportswriters had tagged the Giant Killer.

"He can keep a beat and pitch a ball," one of the men said.

The other man laughed. Not a kind laugh, but a menacing, deriding scoff, causing his friend to look over with surprise.

"You've not heard?" the second man asked.

His friend shook his head.

The scoffing friend went on to explain how Coveleski had been courting a girl and invited her to a concert at which he was performing. When his turn came for a drum solo, and all the other members of the band were looking at him, he was looking down, unaware that he had missed his cue. Apparently, he had thought his solo was later in the performance.

At the time, William sympathized with the pitcher, understanding the frustration and humiliation that could accompany being musically challenged, but the whole event would prove fruitful for William.

Early in the '09 season, the first time the Giants played the Phillies, McGraw had told the team to abuse Coveleski on the mound, to shout embarrassing remarks about his habit of keeping bologna in his back pocket for a snack to ensure he didn't tire in the late innings. It seemed to William that it was a desperate attempt by McGraw to get even for the three losses the Giants had suffered late in the '08 season. But if Little Napoleon was so desperate to resort to bologna-in-the-back-pocket humiliation, perhaps the story of a missed drum solo might somehow be used to the team's advantage. So, William shared the story with McGraw, just before the game started.

The bologna comments shouted by the players seemed to irritate Coveleski, but not to the extent of affecting his performance. Late in the first inning, while Coveleski was in the midst of his windup, McGraw shouted from the third base coaching box, "Rat-a-tat-tat!"

Coveleski pitched wide. He looked over at McGraw with an anger in his face that had a hint of surprise and curiosity. McGraw began a pantomime act of playing a drum.

By the end of the inning, most of the Giants players were shouting or singing, "Rat-a-tat-tat!" along with McGraw.

They hit Coveleski hard.

He was removed in the fourth inning.

He couldn't beat the Giants the rest of the season, and William had gained McGraw's confidence.

***

When the parade outside the Pittsburgh hotel ended, William walked toward the stadium. Everyone on the street, it seemed, greeted one another, waving or shaking hands or stopping to talk or pat each other on the shoulder. It reminded William of New York during the month of December. During the other eleven months, strangers passed one another as if they were angry at people they did not even know, but as the days grew closer to Christmas, the anger somehow magically transformed itself into a feeling of comradery. It was this feeling William sensed amongst the people he passed on his way to Forbes Field.

While he was several blocks from the stadium, he saw a long line of fans winding around Forbes Avenue, down Bouquet, and toward Joncaire. He was relieved that he already had his ticket but felt anxious because the noise was getting louder and the fans were wearing less of the comradery look and more of the angry look.

He reached inside his pocket and touched the envelope that held his ticket. If he had not become the favorite bat boy of the team, he would have never been able to come to the Series in Pittsburgh. Even McGraw had assisted when he learned of William's hope of attending. He contacted the hotel to ensure that William was welcomed and not questioned when he arrived by himself with no adult.

And it was not just the games. So much else would have been different in his life. So much had changed.

Some of the Giants key players had left. Joe McGinnity had retired. Luther Taylor's contract had not been renewed. William missed him, not only because he was the one responsible for the job William held with the Giants, but because he was funny and kind and smart. Luther would laugh his awkward laugh at the vaudeville theaters the team often attended. Most of the other players could also sign, so they were able to interpret the humor for Luther in the midst of the acts, but William's signing skills were more advanced, so Luther grew to rely on his interpretations more than his teammates'.

William went to the library each day after work, reading any book he thought might impress Sir Thomas. When Luther saw him reading, they signed with one another. Most of the books Luther had already read, so William appreciated his insight. The pitcher did not deserve the nickname he had been given by writers and fans—Dummy Taylor was not appropriate for a man of Luther's intelligence.

A new player had arrived, a player who was just as intelligent as Luther and who had also been given a nickname William thought unfair. John Meyers had attended Dartmouth College but left to pursue his baseball career. There were rumors of a forged high school diploma that resulted in his expulsion from the school, but William chose to believe he left to pursue a professional career behind the plate. He had been raised in Riverside, California, and was part Shoshone. Writers and fans referred to Meyers as Chief Meyers. Two other ball players had the same nickname: Albert "Chief" Bender of the Athletics and John "Chief" Wilson of the Pirates. Though William never heard the catcher complain, he recalled that first game in New York during the '05 World Series when the fans were shouting at Chief Bender, causing Sir Thomas's friend to whisper something to the most vocal of the fans. William thought often of this occurrence and the look of shame that overtook the once rabid fan.

But perhaps the greatest difference that season was the change in Matty. It wasn't that Christy Mathewson stopped being a great pitcher. In fact, he had won twenty-five games and lost only six, giving up only a little over one run per game. He was still the best pitcher in either league. But when the team arrived at the clubhouse a few days before the season began, just back from spring training in Marlin, Texas, William did not see the usual hop in Matty's walk. Although he still smiled when he said hello, the corners of his mouth did not rise to the heights they once did. After one of his early wins, Matty gave William his customary one-dollar tip, but rather than saying anything upon his departure from the clubhouse, Matty laid his hand atop William's head, patted it several times, then softly touched his shoulder and walked out.

In late May William learned the likely cause for this change. During the off-season in mid-January, at the home of his parents, Matty found his youngest brother dead. Nicholas Mathewson had walked into the barn and shot himself.

The T-sheet of Christy Mathewson in William's satchel had statistics of win-loss records, strikeouts, walks, and earned runs. The statistics were impressive and spoke of the greatness of the Giants pitcher. On the other side of the sheet, at the top were listed the below-average statistics of Matty's rookie season. Directly underneath was a short record of his performance and loss in the final game of the 1908 season against the Cubs. Underneath those, William added the Mathewson family tragedy of January 15, 1909.

As William waited to enter Forbes Field, the crowd thickened. Fans waiting at the ticket windows acted more desperate than those waiting to be let through the gates. Again, he felt grateful that Matty and others on the team had told McGraw about William's never missing a game of the World Series. On the last day of the season, McGraw handed William an envelope. The note inside read, *Enjoy. Stay safe. Come back with useful information about them bums from Pittsburgh.* Behind the note was a twenty-dollar bill and seven tickets—one to each game.

William reached into his pocket. He smiled and sighed and felt he was the luckiest kid in the country.

Suddenly, a commotion at the front of the line caught his attention. A man had walked straight past William, struggling to push through the crowd.

"Hey, buster!" one of the fans yelled. "Who do you think you are?"

Another shouted, "Yeah! Can't you see there's a line!"

"You gotta wait like the rest of us!"

The fans congregated around the man, not allowing him to reach the front gate.

But William recognized the man. "Hey!" he shouted, surprising himself, fearful that he was now the center of attention. "That's Deacon Phillippe!" William yelled even louder, hoping to alert the fans that they were keeping one of their favorite players from entering the stadium.

It took several seconds, but the crowd soon realized that William was correct. Fans began to step aside, creating a path to the main gate, patting Phillippe on the back and wishing him good fortune. As Phillippe entered, William again felt like the luckiest kid, remembering all that he and Sir Thomas had done six years earlier.

From all the articles William had read, it seemed most of the sportswriters agreed that if the Pirates pitchers had been healthy back in '03, they would have beaten Boston. This year Pittsburgh's big three hurlers were healthy: Howie Camnitz, a twenty-five-game winner; Vic Willis, winning twenty-two; and Lefty Leifield, posting nineteen wins. If the Tigers were to avoid losing their third consecutive championship, they'd have to figure out how to beat the big three.

Yet none of these were on the hill in the first. Instead, the rookie Babe Adams straddled the top of the mound. This choice by Pittsburgh's manager confused William. And he was sure that he was not the only one scratching his head at Forbes.

Adams's first pitch sailed just over the head of the Tigers leadoff hitter, Davy Jones. It took all of George Gibson's agility to catch the ball and keep it from hitting home plate umpire, Johnstone, in the face. The next three pitches were wide. Jones walked to first.

The next batter was Donie Bush. His diminutive stature was immediately publicized by fans shouting "Kiddo" and "Midget" and "Tike" as Detroit's shortstop stepped to the plate. William immediately liked Bush and thought if someone that small could make it to the World Series, then maybe he could also. William inched up in his seat, quietly rooting for Bush to do something well. He laid a perfect bunt down the first base line. It was fielded by Abstein, the Pirates first sacker, and tossed to Miller, covering first. William smiled and leaned back, content that Bush represented small people well.

Cobb was up next. He took a called strike, then walked on the next four pitches.

Crawford hit a hard grounder up the middle, but Pittsburgh's rookie pitcher snagged it just before it passed by him and threw Jones out at third.

Babe Adams had walked two batters and stopped a hard-hit ball up the middle. Still, he was only one out away from getting out of an ugly top of the first. Tigers second baseman, Jim Delahanty, hit a clean single that scored Cobb, giving the Tigers the early lead, and Delahanty took second on the throw home. George Moriarty, the Tigers third baseman, was the next batter. He hit a hard grounder in the hole between short and third, on its way into left field, sure to give Detroit a two-run lead, but the ball struck Delahanty. No run was scored, and the inning was over. Umpire Johnstone raised his right hand, shouting, "Runner's interference! Three outs!"

As the Tigers took the field and the Pirates hitters settled into their dugout, William knew that the Tigers had squandered a golden opportunity. What intrigued William was the curious thought that entered his mind as the Pirates leadoff man, Bobby Byrne, was swinging three wooden bats between his dugout and home plate. "What if," William thought, "somehow the Tigers could use that bad luck in the first inning to their advantage?"

Isn't that what Coveleski had done? Beating the Giants late in the year after they humiliated him in the third game of last season?

Isn't that what Matty did after the 1900 season?

William considered how he had fared in light of the tragedies in his short life, especially following Sir Thomas's death. He had found work and a place to live, found a friend in Chicago, and become a confidant of the great Mugsy McGraw.

While the Tigers pitcher, George Mullin, was retiring the Pirates in order in the bottom of the first, William's mind wandered. He had grown fascinated by the beautiful buildings outside of Forbes, far beyond the outfield grass, and looked into the overcast sky, thinking of not only his good fortune with the Giants but also the surprise that Mr. Danielson, his boss at the Newsboys Home, wanted him to return even after he had left his responsibilities to attend the Series one year earlier. "You are bottled for this job, Mr. Jennings," he had said. "You are hardworking, you are intelligent, you are honest. I will make you a deal. I will allow you to attend the Series each year if you promise to return to this Home and deliver our papers upon your return.

"And furthermore, because of your additional income from the Polo Grounds, your savings is much greater than the other boys. I want you to have an account all your own. At a bank, not in a wooden box at the Home. An actual account at the bank, in your name, your name only. And I will show you how and what to do."

William remembered staring at his employer, not understanding all he said. But in hindsight, he now understood that the trust he had gained from Danielson, the bank account he now knew how to handle on his own, the familiarity he had gained with the bank employees—all this was just as amazing, if not surpassing, the good fortune of being the bat boy for the New York Giants.

Mullin shut down the first nine Pirates he faced. In the bottom of the fourth, he retired the next two. Then Fred Clarke, the Pirates manager and left fielder, hit a long fly ball that soared over the head of Cobb in right, tying the game at one. The Pirates scored two in the fifth, one more in the sixth, and beat the Tigers, 4–1. After that first inning, Babe Adams dominated Detroit. The Tigers had indeed squandered their first-inning opportunity. For the third year in a row, they trailed in the Series, one game to nothing.

Davy Jones walked, opening game two. Shorty Bush sacrificed him to second. Jones was thrown out by Gibson, trying to steal third, knocking down the Pirates third baseman as he slid into the bag. Cobb grounded to second, and Miller fielded and threw to Abstein for the third out.

William looked in dismay as Byrne and Leach, the first two hitters in Pittsburgh's lineup, scored on Miller's ground-rule double. His head cupped in his hands, he lifted his gaze upward toward the outfield as the scoreboard boy lifted the metal plate painted with a bold white *0* and replaced it with the plate painted with a *2*.

He had hoped Detroit would perform better than they had the previous two years. But again, they had lost the first game and were not looking to change course in the early part of game two.

Was it possible to get bored at a ball game?

A World Series game?

He frowned and shut his eyes.

His mind wandered to events occurring a year earlier.

*****

One year ago the Tigers lost to the Cubs. One year ago after the Series had ended, he got lost in Shamokin on his way to Scranton. One year ago he got off the train in Scranton and wandered the streets, hoping to find the location of the law practice, Jennings & Jennings. A librarian at Washington Heights had finally discovered some piece of information about the name on the calling card. And now he was determined to locate the attorneys.

When he first arrived in Scranton, he wasn't sure where to start. All the businesses were closed since the train arrived prior to seven. But he smelled bread nearby, followed the scent, and found a bakery. The man behind the counter read the card William handed him. "The only Jennings business I know in Scranton is the furniture store."

William walked to the store, waited for it to open, and asked if any of them knew Thomas Kemp. None did. A salesman suggested he inquire at the courthouse, directing him to walk two blocks north. The lady at the front desk read the card, holding it far from her eyes, then close, as if she were having difficulty reading the fine print. "Jennings and Jennings," she read. "They are attorneys at law."

She handed the card back to William and smiled. "You'll find them at the pub. Across from the statue of General Washington."

William looked behind him and pointed to his left. "That way?"

She nodded, her smile growing large. "You have a pen in that bag, sweetie?" she asked.

He narrowed his eyes, wondering why she might ask such a question. He reached inside the satchel and held up one of two pens Mr. Danielson had given him as a Christmas present.

The lady nodded. "Very good."

It was as though she were amusing herself that a young boy was looking for an attorney. He put the pen back into the satchel and walked quickly toward the center of town, past the statue of George Washington and to the row of pubs facing him on Linden Street.

He walked into the first pub, on the corner of Washington and Linden, and showed the card to the man behind the bar. He read it and smiled. "That way," he said, as he pointed left.

William's excitement grew, but he forgot to ask the man at which of the remaining pubs on Linden he might find the attorneys. What's more, the man was smiling, like the lady at the courthouse.

The next establishment was closed, the door locked. He looked to the third pub on Linden, where he saw a man sitting next to the window, with papers scattered across the table. His head was down as he read a large book, flipping pages and writing onto a notepad.

William entered quietly through the door and handed the card to the man behind the bar.

"W," the bartender said, loud enough for the man near the window to look up. "You've got a client."

The bartender handed the card back to William.

William turned and looked at the man near the window.

The man the bartender called *W* had large, observant eyes. When he looked up, William felt a burning in his chest. Had he made a mistake searching for this man? He didn't seem impatient. He didn't seem curious. But he did seem important and this made William feel inadequate to disrupt his studies.

William looked back at the bartender, wondering if it was okay for him to approach the booth. The bartender smirked, similar to the expressions William had seen on the faces of the other barkeep and the lady at the courthouse, then motioned with his hand, pointing toward W.

"Well?" W asked. "Let's see what you have there."

William shuffled forward.

W held out his hand and William handed it to him.

W read the card and looked up. "Have a seat. My brother will be here soon."

W returned to the large book and made notations on the pad of paper.

Several minutes passed, William struggling to control his excitement and fear over the uncertainty of who this stranger might be and why they had to wait for his brother before they could proceed.

W reached inside his vest pocket and looked at his watch. He folded his hands atop the large book. "What's your name?" he asked William.

"William Jennings," he answered.

W grinned. Then smiled. And laughed.

"You are now the third William Jennings with whom I have been acquainted," he announced.

William looked up and said nervously, not wanting to speak out of turn, "You mean . . . the senator? Mr. Bryant?"

W nodded. "That's right. He's one of the three."

William felt a bit more relaxed. "Then there's me, I suppose."

"Yes."

"And who's the third?"

W stood and held out his hand. "William Jennings. We've got the same name, young man."

Just then the front doors of the pub opened, and in walked a thin, spritely, redheaded man who looked familiar.

W's eyes widened, "And this is my brother," he announced. "Hugh Ambrose."

***

Almost a year ago to the day, William had shaken the hand of Hugh Ambrose Jennings. For the two previous championships, he had witnessed him suffer defeat at the hands of the Cubs. But now, in the top of the second inning, after the first two Tigers had made outs, George Moriarity and Tom Jones, Detroit's first sacker, each singled. Boss Schimdt, Detroit's light-hitting catcher, clubbed the ball to deep center, almost into the crowd, with Tommy Leach chasing after it. By the time Leach reached the ball and threw it back to Wagner, Detroit had tied the game.

In the third base coach box, Hugh Ambrose Jennings was in the midst of one of his high-kicking celebrations. His left leg was raised high, at a right angle, while he kept his balance on his right leg. Holding this pose, he cupped his hands over his mouth and shouted, "Ee-yah!" He hopped in the air, switching the leg on which he balanced, and shouted even louder, "Ee-yah! Ee-yah!"

In the third, after an error, a single, a base on balls to Cobb, and a base hit by Jim Delahanty, Detroit scored another two runs, and Cobb was standing at third, next to his kicking and yelling and clapping manager. William stood as he cheered and laughed along with those around him. The Pirates manager, Fred Clarke, was not amused. He marched to the mound, removed his best pitcher, Howie Camnitz, and replaced him with Vic Willis. On the first pitch Willis threw, Cobb stole home. The Tigers were leading, 5–2, and the kicking and clapping and shouting from the third base box grew wilder.

William lost count of the number of kicks as Detroit's manager performed his alternating leg celebrations, shouting numerous *ee-yah*'s. The spectacle of a grown man (the field general of the best team in the American League!) displaying such joy over scoring runs at the expense of the home team did not seem to upset any of the Pittsburgh fans. Not even the Pirates players looked annoyed. Some were even smiling.

A grown man acting like a child on the playing field was odd and humorous, but seeing him dressed in a suit, looking like one of the Wall Street executives who daily purchased papers from William, was stunning.

***

"Now," Hugh Ambrose said, turning toward William, "what would you like me to sign?"

His red hair seemed brighter, perhaps because he was up close. His freckles made him look like a little boy. Yet his tweed suit, pants, jacket, and matching vest disguised his playful character. He was carrying a briefcase similar in size and color to the case resting on the chair next to W.

"You're Hughie Jennings!" William gasped.

The brothers looked at one another.

"You are not seeking a signature?" Hughie looked down at William.

W walked back to his chair and sat. He looked up at Hughie. "The young man arrived a few minutes ago. I assumed he was waiting for you."

Still holding the calling card, W held it up toward his brother.

"Where did you get this?" Hughie asked.

"It belonged to Thomas Kemp."

"Brother Thomas Kemp?"

"Yes, sir."

"And you are, then, William John Jennings?"

To hear someone as important as Hughie Jennings say his name as though he mattered caused William to giggle. He covered his mouth. "Yes, sir, that's me."

Immediately, Hugh Ambrose Jennings clapped his hands, pirouetted, kicked his left leg in the air, held it, switched legs, and shouted, "Ee-yah!"

W stared at his brother. "So, he *was* here for you."

Hughie rushed to a chair, placed his briefcase on the table, opened it, and took out a large stack of papers and a thin envelope.

"I've been trying to send these to the school for over a year, and they keep sending them back. *No longer resides at St. Mary's*, the note said with the last returned package."

"Sit," Hughie instructed William.

William obeyed.

Hughie was thumbing through papers, placing one atop the other. "Brother Kemp was a good friend," he said, then looked up once he stopped flipping pages.

"Before he got sick, he asked me to write up his will, explain how to distribute his belongings if anything should happen. He wanted you to have these."

Hughie handed him the folder and some of the pages he had placed in a pile apart from the others. Inside the folder was a stack of Sir Thomas's T-reports. William thumbed through them, reading some names he did not recognize, but many he did— Albert Spalding, Charles Comiskey, Cap Anson, Cy Young.

He looked up at Hughie. "These are mine?"

The redheaded, freckled-faced skipper of the Tigers nodded and held out in his hand a thin envelope, inviting William to take that also.

"Not sure what's inside," Hughie said after William had taken the envelope. "Brother Kemp wanted to make sure you received it. 'Very important for the boy,' he told me."

William looked up at Hughie, hoping he could shed some light as to what might be inside, but Hughie's expression showed no knowledge of its contents. What's more, the writing on the outside of the envelope was the writing of Sir Thomas. It read, *To be opened by William John Jennings – St. Mary's, Baltimore, Maryland.* The envelope was sealed and clearly had never been opened.

Whatever was inside, only he and Sir Thomas would know.

***

The Tigers had tied the Series and were off for Detroit. William boarded the same train as the teams and arriving late in the evening, went straight to his hotel.

He watched five of the first six Pirates cross home plate in the first inning of game three. The Pirates pitcher, Nick Maddox, was making quick work of Detroit: four hits and no runs through the first six innings.

Between the sixth and seventh, William reached into the innermost pocket of the satchel, found the envelope he had received one year earlier from the Tigers manager, and began reading it for the umpteenth time.

Dear William,

Why do you like the stories I read to you each evening? What's more, why do I like them? And what made those stories popular in the first place, that some company would pay money to publish the story? Was it not that thousands, yea, millions of people like you and me also discovered something in the pages that made them feel they were not alone?

The stories speak to us, William, because the characters emerge from problems. We root for them, and we want them to win. The power of the stories is in the similarity they have with the days we live in our world—the problems you and I face.

You have already overcome so much, William, and I am proud of you. I don't suppose I have yet said this to you in spoken words (and if you are reading this letter without ever hearing me say these words, I apologize), but I am proud of you, William. I am proud of knowing William John Jennings.

This letter is part of what we grown-ups call estate planning. It is a way to try to make things easier for those who still live after we are gone. As I write the letter, I have no reason to believe that you will be reading it any time in the near future. It gives me some comfort to think that I have plenty of time to say to you face-to-face the words I wrote in the earlier paragraph. However, I did not want to forgo the opportunity to say in this letter what I hope to someday speak to you about when you are older. In particular, what I know about you: where you came from, where you were born, the circumstances of your birth.

To begin, I do not know much. I will tell you what I know.

You were born on a boat in the Atlantic Ocean, just a few days from arriving in New York Harbor. You were brought to St. Mary's by one of the officers of Ellis Island, my good friend, Alexander Chalmers, who is one of the three men in the picture with me at the Chicago World's Fair. I had hoped for you two to meet when we went to the '05 Series, but he and his family had come down with measles. He is the one who can help you most with questions regarding details of the ship, your parents, and your national origin. His address is 103 Orchard Street in New York City.

My greatest wish is that you never read this letter, that I am able to take the train to Manhattan with you, maybe when you reach your twelfth or thirteenth birthday, and I can introduce you to Alexander and his family. But our stories are unpredictable, William, just like the characters in the stories we like to read. If something horrible has happened, try to remember all we have read, all you have learned. Know that the other brothers at St. Mary's love you. Trust them as I hope you have learned to trust me. Above all, William, try to learn and try to seek and try to trust the one who created you and me and all those you encounter.

And just in case you didn't read it clearly the first time, I am proud of William John Jennings.

Love,

Sir Thomas

***

The Tigers made a valiant comeback effort, scoring four runs in the bottom of the seventh and another two in their half of the ninth. But they came up short, losing 8–6. The Pirates took a 2–1 lead in the Series.

The following day was cold, blistering cold. Fans were wearing ulsters, and many brought blankets. Still, they shivered from the near-freezing temperature and the biting wind blowing across Lake Erie. Detroit took an early lead in the second, scoring two runs, then scored another two in the fourth. Meanwhile, Tigers pitcher George Mullin was pitching a shutout, having given up only two hits over the first five innings. William looked across the expanse of fans. He guessed there were at least fifteen thousand, a good number for such poor weather. Most had come prepared for the cold. But he had not. His teeth were clacking as though he were a telegraph sending code along with the sportswriters sitting above him to their home papers.

He tried to find distractions. The Tigers were creating enough excitement in the bottom innings. They had seven hits and five runs, but the Pirates half-innings were painful. The at bats seemed to take forever, with batters fouling pitches. Six strikeouts meant longer at bats, and longer at bats meant more exposure to the cold, and more cold exposure meant more teeth chattering.

Before the game began, William spotted BJ near the Tigers dugout. As American League president, BJ not only had the best seat at Bennett Park, but he also looked every bit the part of a dignitary, with a plush coat, scarf, vest, and rounded felt hat. It was the coat that William found most amusing. For as circuslike as it may have appeared on a man the size of Ban Johnson, it did look very warm, and William imagined the comfort and warmth he might feel if he owned such a piece of clothing.

William rubbed his hands over his arms, wishing he had purchased a warmer coat, one that had one-tenth the lining that BJ's was sure to have. He grew more conscious of his clicking teeth. The rhythm of the chattering took him back several months to when he sat on a park bench on the Lower East Side of Manhattan, across the street from the house at 103 Orchard Street.

***

It was an early spring day. The weather was warm, and his teeth were chattering as though there had been a January snow. The Giants were on the road, so William had the afternoon free. He had done what had become a habit over the last two months whenever time allowed. He would sit on the bench and watch the comings and goings of the house on Orchard Street. The problem was that so many people entered the bottom floor of the building, and the building was six stories tall. There were two doors near the front of the building: one that seemed to lead to the home on the bottom floor, and one that opened to the stairs leading to the other homes. He did not know on which floor Sir Thomas's friend lived. For two months he had hoped to recognize the face of one of the four men in Sir Thomas's picture, but most of the grown-ups returned home after the sun had set, so it was difficult to make out facial features in the darkening streets.

William finally decided that he would knock on the front door of the home on the bottom floor, hoping that whoever answered would know Sir Thomas's friend.

That particular early spring afternoon, he sat on the bench for only a few minutes before he decided to knock. His anxiety almost kept him from walking toward the front steps.

He raised his hand, hesitated for several seconds, then knocked once.

Nobody answered.

He knocked again. Still no answer.

He heard several high-pitched voices. He heard footsteps. He heard the metal doorknob jiggle.

He looked down at the knob and saw it turn.

The door opened.

William looked up.

"Yes?" a young man asked.

He was a few years older than William, taller and broader. His thick brown hair was parted to the side, and his face looked like it needed a shave.

William stuttered. "I'm here for . . . I mean to say, I'm looking for . . ."

He knew the name, had rehearsed this encounter while trying to fall asleep, but somehow the anxiety he felt erased the name from his memory.

He reached into his pocket and took out Sir Thomas's letter.

"Does Alexander Chalmers live here?"

***

The Tigers had tied the Series again, two games each. The teams boarded the trains, and the cold weather followed the teams to Pittsburgh for game five. Davy Jones led off with a home run, belting Babe Adams's fastball over the head of center fielder Tommy Leach. But Pittsburgh tied the game in the bottom of the inning, then scored another run in the second and again in the third, taking a 3–1 lead into the sixth. Cobb's single, Crawford's double, and an error by Honus Wagner plated another two runs for Detroit. After the Pirates added a run, they were up by one going to the bottom of the seventh. Despite the discomfort of the cold, the game's back-and-forth was keeping William from the discomfort he felt in Detroit.

Then the Pirates' bats heated up. Byrne led off with a single, smashing the ball between short and third. Leach hit another hard grounder through the same hole, and Clarke hit a three-run home run, giving the Pirates a four-run lead. Wagner was hit by a pitch, stole second, then stole third. The catcher threw the ball into left field, trying to throw out Wagner, allowing Honus to score on the error. The Pirates were up by five. Though Crawford hit a home run in the top of the eighth, William felt the game was out of reach, and his thoughts wandered outside of Forbes's foul lines, into the memories of the house on Orchard Street.

***

"Alexander Chalmers?" the young man repeated.

William nodded, his hopes rising, for it seemed the young man spoke the name with confidence, as though it was a name he recognized.

"Alexander Chalmers?" the young man repeated once more. "Well, yes, that's me, but most people call me Eli, my middle name. Eli, Eli Chalmers, or Alexander Elimelech Chalmers. But you can call me Eli."

The young man was smiling. He had stepped aside and swept his arm through the air, inviting William to enter.

William walked through the doorway and looked up at Eli. He hadn't realized how tall his host was when he first opened the door. Originally, William had thought he was only one or two years older. Now he wasn't sure.

"Can I take your coat?" Eli asked.

William shook his head.

"Your bag? You can set over there if you like, by the table."

William looked to the ground, raised the satchel to his chest, and shook his head once more.

Eli walked toward the table. It appeared to be a dinner table, much like the ones eight to ten of the boys at St. Mary's would sit at for each meal. Beyond the table was a doorway, though there was no door, and through the doorway William saw a stove and a wall on which pots and pans and spoons hung from nails.

He turned in the other direction, from which high-pitched children's voices were chattering. On the floor, two girls each held a rag doll. They were pantomiming, as though the dolls were puppets. They appeared to be putting on a show for a young boy, who was clapping and giggling. Against the wall in a crib was a toddler pulling himself, or herself, up by using the top rail of the crib for leverage. The toddler fell on its bottom, then started making the effort once more.

"Come, sit," Eli invited.

William sat at the side of the table facing the doorway that appeared to lead to the kitchen. He unstrapped the satchel from his shoulder and set it on his lap. He shifted in his seat, looking back at the children. The toddler had just fallen and was reaching once more for the railing.

As William wondered at the toddler's tenacity and admired, even envied, the enjoyment of the other children, two items caught his attention. Hanging side by side on the wall several feet above the toddler and the crib was a plain bronze cross, similar to the cross in the chapel at St. Mary's. Next to it was a shiny metal star, the two-triangle star that William recalled first seeing at the Jewish synagogue of Sir Thomas's friend.

"I imagine," Eli said, as he sat across from William, "that you are here to see my father."

William turned.

"Is your name William Jennings?" Eli asked.

William was startled. And nodded.

Eli stood and touched William's right shoulder. "Wait here," he instructed.

Eli went into the kitchen. William heard him open a cabinet, then heard him open something like a jar or container. Several seconds later, Eli returned and handed William an envelope.

Another envelope!

William looked down at the letter. The beads of sweat on his palms had soiled the envelope and slightly smudged the letters on the outside, which read, *William John Jennings*.

"And there's this," Eli announced as he extended both arms, cradling in his palms a neatly folded thick white blanket. "Papa told us it belongs to you."

William extended his arms, receiving the blanket. It appeared mostly white, but William could see there was stitching—intricate stitching that created some sort of scene. He wanted to stand up, unfurl the blanket, and examine it further, but he had a more pressing question on his mind.

He wanted to ask about Eli's father, but he sensed some explanation would be forthcoming for why he was receiving a letter instead of meeting Alexander Chalmers.

"Our father passed away a couple years ago," Eli said softly. "Thus the letter."

Eli's eyes were lowered. William nodded, grateful for Eli's explanation without William having to ask.

William lowered his head, again reading his name on the envelope. Then he looked up at Eli, turned his head and observed the children, now playing quietly with their toys.

He wanted to open the letter. But not in this house in which he was a stranger. He wanted to read it and read it and read it again.

He wanted the freedom to cry and shout and yell and ask for help from that person or thing that created him and Sir Thomas and all the others. He reached out and placed his hand on the blanket, rubbing his right palm over the surface, finding some comfort in the softness and the feel of its welcoming warmth. If the blanket was to be his, then he would take it with him, pack it securely in his satchel. He wondered if he could make it fit. As he began to push it inside the satchel's main compartment, he felt someone nudge his left arm.

He turned his head.

The little boy was there. He nudged William again, but this time with more force.

"You know my friend?" the boy asked.

William was confused. He shrugged and looked toward Eli, imagining the boy was Eli's younger brother, and hoping that Eli could offer some clarification. But Eli looked curious, as though he was as confused as William.

The two girls were standing behind the boy, both giggling and holding the dolls with which they were playing moments earlier. And as they continued their giggling, William recognized that the girls looked like one another—not in one feature, not just their hair color or height or facial features, but in every respect. They were perfect replicas. And what made William smile inside more than anything was that he could not imagine that there could exist a more perfect being of whom there ought to be an exact copy.

They were beautiful!

Again, the boy nudged him, but this time it was with a closed fist. "My friend has a twin brother, just like I have twin sisters. Maybe you'll recognize them?"

Now the boy raised both arms and clenched both fists. He took a small step back with his right foot and waited. "Now do you recognize them?"

William was unsure how to respond. The girls were still giggling. Their little brother appeared serious.

Eli clapped his hands once loudly and stood. "David, William is our guest. There will be no fighting guests in our home today."

David kept his arms raised and began to dance, shuffling his feet as if to find the best attacking point against William.

Eli walked to his sisters, standing behind them and facing William. He placed his hands atop their heads as David danced back toward the crib and shadowboxed near his younger sibling.

Eli raised his right hand. "This is Naomi," he announced, and placed his hand atop one sister's head. He rested his left hand on his other sister. "This is Mara."

William was about to ask how Eli was able to distinguish one sister from the other when he spotted a red blotch on Mara's right cheek, halfway between her ear and nose.

"And back there," Eli said as he pointed toward the crib, "behind those bars, is Jessica."

David was next to the crib, shuffling his feet, kicking one foot in front of the other, putting on a display before his little sister, pumping his arms as if he were in the ring with her. She raised her arms, giggling, reaching upward, perhaps with hopes that David could help her escape the crib.

"Nap time!" Eli sang out. "Nap time!" He drew out the words. "Nap time for all, nap time in spring, nap time for summer, nap time in fall."

David stopped his shadowboxing and fell to the floor at the legs of the crib. Mara and Naomi ran into a back room and returned seconds later, each holding two pillows. Naomi tossed one of the pillows to David, then fell to the floor, lying next to him. Mara ran to William and handed him a pillow, then ran to her siblings, dropped to the floor, and closed her eyes.

"I've got some work to do in the kitchen," Eli said softly to William. "You are welcome to sit at the table, read the letter if you like, ask me any questions about my father. I'll answer what I can."

William accepted the invitation. He sat at the table, this time facing the wall with the cross and the Star of David. The children were already asleep. He placed both hands on the blanket, maneuvering them across the surface, letting the fine shreds tickle his palms.

He picked up the envelope. With his finger he carefully unsealed the flap, then unfolded the letter.

***

The memories of the past year had lulled William into a stupor, and he suddenly realized the game had ended. Forbes Field was mostly empty, and he was one of the few fans still sitting.

He looked to the scoreboard—the Pirates had held on to win, 8–4. They were one win away from making up for their loss to the Red Sox six years earlier. The Tigers were one loss away from losing their third consecutive World Series. The teams boarded their trains for Detroit.

Game six started well for Pittsburgh. Their first three batters—Byrne, Leach, and Clark—all scored, thanks in large part to Wagner's double, but by the fourth inning the game was tied. And after Detroit scored single runs in the fifth and sixth, it looked like the Series was going to be knotted up at three games each.

In the top of the ninth, with Detroit up 5–3, Dots Miller led off with a clean single. Bill Abstein singled.

Chief Wilson bunted. Catcher Boss Schmidt fielded the ball cleanly, but rushing his throw to first, he threw wide, making it necessary for Tom Jones to leave his regular fielding position at first, and colliding with Wilson, Jones was knocked unconscious. For fifteen minutes medical staff worked on the Tigers first baseman. A gurney was brought onto the field, and Jones was carried off. Miller had scored. The score was 5–4. Pirates had men on first and second, with nobody out.

The Tigers' hope of success seemed to mirror the cards William had been dealt. As the medical staff cared for the Tigers first baseman, William looked on, reciting the opening words written by Alexander Chalmers. As he mouthed the opening lines of the letter, he reached into his satchel, thumbed past Sir Thomas's letter, and opened the letter he had received several months earlier from Eli.

***

Dear Mr. Jennings,

I met you on the morning of Friday, June 11, 1897, just days after you were born. The precise day of your birth was unknown to me then, and I imagine we'll always be uncertain as to the exact day of your birth. This is not from any lack of effort. Many people spent days attempting to determine as much detail about you as was possible. These details I will share with you shortly.

I had hoped to speak with you face-to-face, give you an opportunity to ask questions, and possibly assist you in finding more answers, but when my doctor informed me that the tuberculosis I had contracted was of a serious nature, I immediately tried to contact Brother Kemp and inform him of the situation. This was during the fall of '06. And I learned from the telegram I received back from the other brothers that you and he were in Chicago for the Series between the Cubs and Sox. My health was deteriorating quickly. This letter is the best I could do, trying to ensure that some information of your history could be communicated to you.

***

William looked up from the letter as the crowd began to awaken from the shock of watching one of their beloved Tigers carried off the field.

Detroit still held a modest lead when Pirates catcher George Gibson hit a hard single into center, sure to tie the score at five, but Sam Crawford fielded the ball cleanly and fired it home to Boss Schmidt, who caught the throw and applied the tag on Abstein just as Abstein arrived at the plate. Another collision hushed the cheering fans. Schmidt held onto the ball, but during the collision, the Pirates first baseman's spikes gashed Schmidt's leg.

Tigers still held a one-run lead, but at what price? Their first baseman had been carried off the field on a stretcher. Two minutes later, their catcher's leg was gushing with blood.

Again, medical staff interrupted the game.

William looked back at the letter and continued reading.

***

On the evening of June 9, you were discovered on a ship traveling from Europe. The boat was named the Noorlander, and it traveled back and forth several times each year, transporting immigrants from Europe and vacationers from America, between Antwerp and New York Harbor. The medical staff at Ellis Island determined that the earliest your mother could have given birth was on the evening of Sunday, June 6, and the latest on Tuesday, June 8. We decided to place June 7 on your birth certificate, feeling it made the most sense.

We made every effort to discover who your mother might be. The ship's manifest recorded the same number of expectant mothers boarding the ship in Antwerp as disembarked in New York. We determined that your mother was not one of those waiting to be processed at the immigration station. The same sailor who found you had minutes earlier witnessed a woman fall from the ship into the water, but he was unable to save her. We believe this woman was your mother. We believe she didn't fall accidentally. It appears she jumped on her own volition.

***

Play on the field resumed, and William folded the letter, placed it in the envelope, and slipped it back in the satchel.

The Tigers still held a one-run lead in the top of the ninth. With one out and men on first and second, Pittsburgh's Wilson broke for third in attempt of a double steal. During his slide into the third base bag, he collided with Detroit's third baseman, George Moriarty, buckling Moriarty's left knee. Wilson was out. And the Pirates pinch hitter, Ed Abbaticchio, struck out to end the game, giving the Tigers the win and tying the Series at three. But Detroit's first baseman was unconscious, their catcher had a gashed leg, and their third baseman was hobbling, the strength of his knee uncertain.

William walked to his hotel, almost certain that Detroit could not win the next game, almost as certain as the hopelessness of finding answers to his questions.

Sitting on the edge of the bed in his room, he unfolded the letter and continued reading.

***

For the next five days, many of us at the immigration station, including myself, conducted interviews and gathered as much information as we could, hoping for some clues to your mother's identity. Though the Noorlander left from a Belgian port, Antwerp is often the preferred point of departure for many Eastern European and Russian immigrants. For this reason it is very difficult to make any assumption as to your nationality. What makes this determination even more difficult is the fire which occurred on the island the evening of June 15.

Brother Kemp has told me that you are a bright boy. And for this reason I believe you may understand why I feel the fire of June 15 to be irony. A mixed blessing perhaps may be a better way of describing it. You see, the fire destroyed all documents of immigration records. Therefore, all the interviews we performed, including of the crew and passengers of the ship on which you were born, were forever lost. This makes any research you would hope to do impossible. The irony, however, is that the fire enabled us to place you at St. Mary's with relative ease. Without the distraction created by the fire, we may not have had such ease in placing you at St. Mary's.

***

By the second inning of game seven, the Pirates were leading, 2–0. At the end of the fourth, the score was 4–0. After six, it was 7–0. After eight, the score was 8–0. And after nine, the Tigers had lost the World Series for the third year in a row.

***

On the eastbound train from Pittsburgh, William rested his head against the window, his chest and head damning the tears he would not let escape. He had read the letter by Sir Thomas and the letter from Eli's father so often, he had almost memorized them. The logical conclusion was that William was a mistake. He was an intrusion into the lives of his father and mother. So much so that his mother ended her own life.

His value to his world was as small as the Tigers' chances of ever winning a world championship. As much as Sir Thomas may have told him that he was valuable and smart and special, this did not equate with the fact that he was a bastard. He had no family. He was alone.

He recalled the hopelessness he felt after reading Mr. Chalmers's letter the first time. While sitting at the table, with Eli in the kitchen and Eli's siblings taking their naps, he had determined to leave unannounced. He had needed to escape, walk out those doors, find a lonely place to cry, get it out of his system, and vow to never cry again. He would return to his world of selling papers and picking up after grown men who happened to be the best ballplayers in the country. He would find some way to make enough money to show all the others that William John Jennings was important. William John Jennings did exist.

The train whistle awoke many of the passengers in William's car. Many looked up, but quickly closed their eyes, returning to sleep.

But William could not rest—again he replayed that moment he left the house on Orchard Street.

***

He had stuffed the blanket into the satchel, the bulginess of the white wool making it almost impossible to buckle the straps, with fabric protruding from every crevice. He walked slowly to the front door and quietly opened it, stepped out and cautiously closed it, and turned left, walking toward the East River and the mammoth railings of the Williamsburg Bridge.

Already, he felt his heart surging, pumping—seeking a release, a place to lay his head and let the stream of tears escape.

He heard voices all around him, people to whom he knew he held no value, just like all the people he would ever encounter. Perhaps Sir Thomas was different. Perhaps Alexander Chalmers was different too. But they were gone.

Now he heard other voices. Children's voices from behind. They were getting louder, and he could tell by their laughter and cadence of footsteps that they were skipping.

The sound of skipping stopped. Someone brushed up against him and grabbed his right hand, wrapping tiny fingers around his larger, thicker fingers.

He looked down and saw David.

He turned and saw Naomi and Mara brushing the hair of their dolls.

Several feet behind the twin sisters, Eli pushed a stroller from which the youngest of the Chalmers children looked up at her older sisters, turned to look at David, then looked back at her eldest brother. She was squirming, begging, it seemed, to be set loose.

Two weeks after the nation had celebrated the birthday of its first president in '07, before William had left St. Mary's, Brother Michael, William's history teacher, had written on the chalk easel the name of George Washington. To the right of Washington's name he wrote a span of years, *1732–1799*, and next to these he wrote another span of years, *1789–1797*. Above Washington's name Brother Michael wrote *President* and underlined it twice. Above the first span of years he wrote *Lifetime* and underlined it twice. Finally, over the second span of years he wrote *Time in Office*, underlining it as well. He placed the chalk back on the tray, then began a lesson about the Lewis and Clark expedition, not addressing the items he had seconds earlier written on the board.

The next day was the same. He wrote *John Adams*, then in the other two columns he wrote *1735–1826* and *1797–1801*. He placed the chalk on the tray and started a new lesson about the Louisiana Purchase.

On day three, he wrote *Thomas Jefferson, 1743–1826*, and *1801–1809*. Unlike the previous two days, he addressed the purpose of writing the names and announced that the class would be required to memorize not only the order in which the presidents served, but also the spans of their lives and the years they served as president. He added one president each day. By mid-April, all twenty-six names, along with the two columns of years, were listed on the classroom's three blackboards.

William grew fascinated as he learned how the years of each president's lifetime were interconnected with those who served before and after his term in office. He found it intriguing that Grover Cleveland was the only man to serve nonconsecutive terms, serving as both the twenty-second and twenty-fourth Commander-in-Chief; that William McKinley, when he had just turned eighteen, fought in the Civil War, risking his life at the Battle of Antietam to deliver food and supplies to his comrades under heavy fire; and that the British killed Andrew Jackson's family during the Revolution, leaving him an orphan when he was fourteen.

He felt an affinity for Jackson when he learned of his early years and found hope that he too could rise above the lot he had been dealt, perhaps attaining great things like Jackson, who became the nation's greatest hero during the 1812 war and served as president. But there was one particular phenomenon on the list that fascinated William and his classmates more than any other story told them by Brother Michael.

The first day that Brother Michael spoke of the list was day three, after he had written the name and years of Thomas Jefferson.

He asked the students if they noticed anything peculiar about the years of Jefferson's life.

After some silence, one of the brighter boys raised his hand and said, "Jefferson and Adams died the same year."

Brother Michael smiled. "In fact," William recalled him saying, "they died on the same day, July Fourth."

Of all days for two of the founding fathers to die, the fiftieth celebration of the nation's birthday. What was more, the two men who had been political rivals became friends during the later part of their lives and regularly wrote letters to one another. Included in some of their correspondence was the jesting about which of them would outlive the other.

When William learned of Alexander Chalmers's death and that he had written a letter to Sir Thomas days before he lost his battle to tuberculosis, unaware that Sir Thomas was suffering from his own illness, and when he learned that Eli's father died on the evening of October 14, the same day the White Sox completed their World Series victory over the Cubs, the day William sat at Sir Thomas's bedside holding his hand when he stopped breathing, William felt an eerie similarity between the Jefferson-Adams friendship and the friendship and deaths of Eli's father and Sir Thomas.

It made it all seem quite noble, like there was a great purpose to it, that all of them—Eli's father, Sir Thomas, and even William himself—held some importance. Just as Adams and Jefferson played important roles in the history of the nation, the two friends held important roles in William's life. When these thoughts danced in his mind, William shook his head, feeling the thought too wonderful to be true, that an orphan's life could hold any value. Then he'd think of Andrew Jackson. Then he'd reach into the satchel, into the inner side pocket, and take out the picture of Sir Thomas and his three friends. Several months earlier William had dropped the frame, cracking the glass, so he decided to remove the picture and throw the frame away. Now he could store it in the satchel without worrying about how much space it took. Each time he looked at the four faces, he instinctively placed his right hand lightly near the top of Sir Thomas's head, then held the picture carefully on the edges of the photograph. Though he had met Sir Thomas's rabbi friend, he knew for certain that he would not meet Eli's father, and he imagined that he'd not meet the other man, whose name he had forgotten, the one whom he searched out in Chicago but who had moved farther west.

Could friendship be that special? Could friendship be so strong that someone would frame a picture and hang it on a wall or set it on a desk, like you would for members of your family? William's closest friend had been Timmy, but he'd likely never see him again. George and Congo were good friends, but he never felt like he could be as silly around them as he could be with Timmy. Whatever the four men in the picture held in common, it bound a friendship that had lasted almost twenty years. Whenever William looked at the picture, he wondered and hoped to someday have what they shared. And after he met Eli and Eli's siblings, he wondered whether perhaps he, like Sir Thomas, could be a friend of the Chalmers family.

It had been over a year since he met them, a year since the day little David had grabbed his hand and skipped ahead, forcing William to run beside him. Five minutes later they had arrived at a park on the edge of the East River. William climbed trees with David and his twin sisters, and they took turns pushing each other on the swings. Eli sat on a park bench, slowly pushing and pulling the stroller, trying to occupy baby Jessica, attempting in vain to lull her asleep. That evening they invited William to dinner at their home. Eli cooked since their mother and elder sister, Ruth, were still at work and on most nights arrived home long after the children were in bed.

Eli invited William to return the next day. And the next. And the next.

When the Giants were in town, William was not able to visit the family. After finishing the cleaning of the Polo Grounds clubhouse, he didn't have enough time to take the train to the Lower East Side and back to the Newsboys Home before curfew.

By late summer he was visiting at least once each week, but always for supper on Sunday afternoon. As William was leaving after the Sunday meal on September 4, Eli asked him, "Can you make it on Wednesday?"

"Not certain," William answered. "Giants are in town for a long home stand. They're here for most of the month."

Eli scratched his head. "The girls have planned something. Big surprise."

"I'll see what I can do."

William spoke with the house father at the Newsboys Home and received permission to arrive on the evening of the 7th by ten o'clock. He was granted permission by McGraw that a cursory cleaning of the clubhouse would be sufficient after the game on Wednesday, as long as William arrived earlier the next morning to make sure the floors and lockers were clean. William had done everything in his power to make it to the Chalmerses' home in time for dinner and the girls' surprise.

Christy Mathewson, as if he were aware of William's predicament, pitched a six-hit shutout against the Braves. The game was scoreless in the bottom of the eighth, causing William great worry that they were headed for extra frames. But Al Bridwell hit in the first run of the game, and a Braves error allowed the Giants to go ahead by two heading into the ninth. Matty completed his shutout, and the game ended just past 3:30—one of the quickest games of the season. "Thank you, Matty!" William sang to himself as he collected the balls and bats, cleaned the cleats, and swept the clubhouse floor.

It had been a hopeless season for the Giants. Although they had a winning record and were currently in second place, for the past two months they had been double digits behind the league-leading Cubs. Matty was once more performing brilliantly, having just won his twenty-third game with the shutout, but there was little chance the Giants would be playing for the world championship in October.

But today, this held little importance. William changed out of his uniform, put on his street clothes, rushed to the nearest elevated train stop, and headed for the Lower East Side.

When he arrived, Eli opened the door and directed him to sit on the large sofa. Naomi and Mara were sitting in chairs under the cross and the Star of David. They were each dressed in lace, Naomi in a brilliant white gown that fell to her ankles, with black trim on the edge of the sleeves, collar, and train, and Mara in a dress of deep black with white trim. They sat with their arms folded in their laps, neither of them smiling. And this disturbed William, for their smiles were one of the things he had grown to love about the family. Perhaps the girls had been punished and were awaiting the declaration of what their punishment might be.

Then from the back room of the house, David entered.

William constrained his impulse to laugh at David's attire: a black suit that resembled a tuxedo but was not cut exactly like a tuxedo. He was carrying in each hand a black case, each shaped like a violin. He walked toward his sisters and set the cases on the floor at the foot of their chairs.

Naomi and Mara simultaneously reached down to pick up the cases and place them on their laps. In unison, they unlatched the buckles of the cases, removed the instruments, removed the bows and the rosin, closed the cases, and set them back onto the floor.

Still, neither of them smiled.

Uncertain of the quality of sound that would soon emerge from the girls' instruments, William was determined to show respect, not to giggle or look away, but to do whatever had to be done to display his enjoyment of the occasion.

When the first notes played, there was nothing awful about it. It was a simple tune, a tune he recognized, the second melody played by Sir Thomas on the organ the night they met.

Seconds into their performance, the notes played by Naomi and Mara diverged, creating harmony with the melody, enhancing the prettiness of the tune.

The tune lasted two minutes at most. David stood and clapped his hands. Eli stood and clapped with more enthusiasm. William felt paralyzed, awed at the skill of the sisters. He realized his mouth was wide open as he gawked at the girls in wonder, so he jumped to his feet, joining David and Eli in their accolades, hoping to minimize his foolishness.

The sisters played many more tunes. William lost count. Somewhere between the seventh and eighth pieces he shut his eyes, overcome by the exhaustion of the day, the anticipation of making it to the house in time. When he awoke, the room was empty and the chairs were placed back at the supper table. William looked toward the kitchen and heard the four siblings talking softly, clanging kitchen utensils, shuffling across the floor.

The relief William felt upon waking on the sofa, watching Eli and the others preparing dinner, was something he had never experienced. He was happy. He felt that nobody was looking over his shoulder, measuring him, grading him, expecting anything of him. He was no longer a guest in the house. Though he was not a member of the family, they let him fall asleep on the sofa. They left the room and let him sleep. He took a deep breath. Feeling his lungs fill with air confirmed that he was awake. He turned again, watching the movement of shadows in the kitchen, hearing the rattling of metal and porcelain, all to prepare a meal of which he would partake.

When Naomi stepped from the kitchen holding three plates, William saw she was no longer dressed in her white gown but in the play clothes he regularly saw her wear. Behind her, Mara was wearing a brown flannel dress. The sisters placed the plates at the table, followed by David, setting the cups at each place.

After they ate and cleared the table and washed the dishes, the front door opened.

David and the twins raced to the entrance, each waiting to be hugged by their eldest sister.

Ruth placed her purse on the floor. "One for the first," she sang as she knelt and wrapped her arms around David, burrowing her head into his chest. Then, placing her lips on his cheek, she blew air rapidly, vibrating David's face, causing him to giggle.

Ruth shuffled on her knees to Naomi. "Two for the second," she sang in a higher octave, releasing her embrace of Naomi after several seconds, then wrapping her arms around Naomi once more, tightening and squeezing until Naomi squealed.

Ruth shuffled to Mara and stopped. "And three for the last," she sang, again raising the melody higher. She didn't lift her arms immediately, waiting for Mara to make eye contact. Once she did, both Mara and Ruth smiled, and then Ruth embraced her. The second embrace lasted a few moments longer. It seemed to William that the sisters were in a world of their own, their eyes closed, Ruth savoring the embrace, and Mara as though she had found the softest pillow in the history of the world. When Ruth released her arms, it was for less than a second, and the final hug was longer, tighter, sweeter than all those William previously witnessed.

Normally, it was only on Sunday afternoons that William saw Ruth. She worked the other six days of the week from six in the morning until eight in the evening. Recently, on Wednesdays and Fridays, she'd been allowed to leave the factory in the late afternoon to attend nursing school. She said she would not miss the garment district once she earned her nursing certificate, but what she would miss was the people with whom she worked, not the work itself. And once she graduated, her greatest joy would be to serve those with whom she once sewed and knitted.

After the final embrace of Mara, Ruth stood and stretched. She raised her arms over her head and moved her head left to right several times, as if she was searching for something or someone.

"Ah, there you are," she said, her eyes focused on William. "Eli said you were coming over this afternoon."

She walked slowly toward William, as if seeking a sign that it was okay to do what she was about to do.

William did not move. And though he thought he tried to remain stoic, he felt the corners of his mouth rise.

"William Jennings," Ruth said as she spread her arms. "Mr. Senator," she continued as she bent down toward him, "request permission to give the honorable Mr. Jennings a hug."

William bowed his head. "Permission granted," he answered softly.

"Hoorah!" David shouted.

The twins giggled, clapping their hands. "He's learning!" Naomi whispered to Mara.

As she drew closer, William felt his pulse quicken. When she bent down, he looked into her hazel-blue eyes and felt his palms moisten. When she placed her arms around his torso, squeezing, so that his head rested on her shoulder and he smelled her and saw up close the thick, rich, blackness of her long hair, he closed his eyes, accepted the embrace, and wished it might not end.

She pulled away, stood straight, and asked William, "How'd you like the girls' performance?"

"It was—" he started, before Mara interrupted.

"He fell asleep," she announced.

"Well, Mara, dear," Ruth said, turning toward her sister, "he slept because your playing was so sweet."

"Like a lullaby!" David shouted.

William looked at Mara, fearful that he had offended her. He looked at Naomi. Both were smiling. Perhaps they were only teasing.

As William struggled with what to say, Eli entered from the kitchen and asked Ruth, "I thought you had class tonight?"

"Mama asked me to check the mail. See if some bills came. And take them to Uncle Nathan."

Eli picked up a stack of letters from the bookshelf behind the supper table. "These?"

Ruth's eyes widened. "Oh, Eli! Please! Take them for me!"

"We are going to the park. Kids have been bugging me all day."

"Drop them off for me. The kids haven't seen Uncle for almost a year. I'll stay here with baby Jesse."

William looked over at the twins and David. David seemed fine, but the twins did not. Naomi was biting her lip. Mara was rubbing the top of her head with her right hand, and with her left she held Naomi's right arm.

"Look at them." Eli pointed toward the twins. "They're terrified of him."

"We all were. They'll warm up."

Ruth turned to David. "What do you think of Uncle Nathan?"

"Hoorah for Uncle Nathan!" David shouted.

Eli shook his head. "He'll say anything about anybody. He just wants to leave. If the most evil man were waiting outside, it wouldn't matter to him, just so we get out those doors. Listen. Hey, David, what do you think of Tammany Hall?"

"Hoorah, Tammy Hall!"

"And Czar Nicholas?"

"Hoorah for the czar!"

"And Robespierre?"

"Hoorah, ropey bear!"

As Ruth walked past Eli, she touched his shoulder and said, "Take the papers, Eli."

***

It was a short walk, just a couple blocks north.

"He's a bit odd," Eli whispered to William as they approached the building at the end of Houston Street. "He's Mama's uncle, not ours. Guess that makes him our grand uncle or something of the sort."

When they arrived, the front door was closed but unlocked. Eli slowly turned the knob and held the door open until everyone entered. Inside, it smelled musty, like the windows had been closed for a long while.

"He's been out West," Eli said as he closed the front door. "Got back a couple days ago."

David raced to a door just to the right of the entrance. "He must be in the workshop!" he said loudly.

As David turned the knob of the door that led to the basement, Eli extended his hand, bracing it on the middle part of the door, keeping it from being opened.

David looked up and frowned.

Eli bowed his head, looking at Naomi, then Mara, then David. Slowly shifting his eyes again from one sibling to the next, he instructed, "Not a sound from your mouths. Understand? He's working. Doesn't want to be disturbed. Take off your shoes. The only sound I want to hear is the muffled *poof, poof, poof* of your feet."

Each of the children obeyed. They lowered themselves to the floor quietly, untied their laces, and removed their shoes. By the stern expression on Eli's face and the unblinking eyes toward William, William understood that he also was to remove his shoes. Finally, Eli unlaced his own shoes and placed them quietly onto the floor.

He turned the knob.

He opened it a crack, maybe an inch. Then another two inches. Then three. Each time, he paused. There were no creaks. This was a relief to William, for he realized he had been holding his breath at each of Eli's movements.

"I'll go first," Eli whispered. "Then David, then the twins. William, you follow."

As they descended, it took several seconds for William's eyes to adjust to the dark. There was light, but it was faint. By the time he made it to the base of the stairs, he could make out the expanse of the room. Numerous lights hung from the ceiling, all very weak, and about fifteen lit candles rested atop bookshelves, worktables, stools, and chairs.

On the far end of the basement, a dark, heavy curtain hung on a large bar held on either side by two equal-sized metal bars. The curtain was partly open, and if it were not for the flicker of low red embers seeping through the seams of the curtain, whatever was behind the curtain would be hidden in total blackness.

Three of the four walls were bare—no pictures, no decoration of any kind. But on the wall leading to the stairwell, a series of photographs hung. William stepped off the bottom stair and examined them.

The photographs were framed and arranged in six rows. The top row was devoted to Ruth, each picture showing her growth from an infant to a young woman. Eli was the subject of the second row. The twins occupied the third and fourth rows, David the fifth, and baby Jesse the sixth.

William turned back toward the others and walked closer to the center of the room.

The floor was all wood, with no rugs. It was clean, painfully clean. In fact, there was no musty smell as there was upstairs. Instead, there was a poignant acidic, chemical-like odor which likely killed any mustiness attempting to infiltrate the basement.

William wasn't sure which was more disturbing—musty or acidic.

There were three wooden tables, each a different size, arranged in the midst of the basement. The largest table was closest to the staircase. Strewn on the floor and on the table was an assortment of tools that William recognized—hammers, saws, and screwdrivers. The far table was smaller than the first and was outside the curtain with the faint red light. Resting on top and on the floor were several containers. They looked to William like the containers used to wash dishes or to give a baby a bath. Next to this table were two tripods, one taller than the other. Each held a different-sized box camera.

Near the center of the basement, seated at the smallest table was a man hunched over, holding a small cylinder-shaped metallic device to his right eye, examining a fragment that rested on a black cloth on the table. At times, the cylinder sparkled. William noticed that when one of the lights on the ceiling made contact with it at just the right angle, the gadget glittered. It seemed to be some type of magnifying instrument. The man picked up the object on the black cloth with a pair of tweezers and held it up, almost touching the glass on one end of the cylinder, studying it with his eye by looking through the other end.

In one hand was the cylinder, and in the other he held the object that glistened and sparkled. William had never seen a diamond, but he was sure that was what the man held. His mind raced back to Sir Thomas and the stories Thomas had read to him at night about the rare stones belonging to French royalty and Napoleon.

The man was dressed in brown pants, brown vest, brown jacket, white shirt, and black suspenders. He looked like what William had always imagined a farmer to look like, though William had never met or seen a live farmer. But until now, he had never seen a diamond either.

The man looked up. He was either resting his eyes or confused by what he had seen in the diamond. He showed no signs that he was aware that others were watching him. He moved his head left to right, shaking it as if to rid his mind of clutter, then placed the cylinder back to his eye, holding the diamond close to the cylinder's other end.

David moved first. He took two steps, stopped, then took two more steps and stopped. He continued, increasing the speed of this routine until he was a couple feet from the table. He placed his hands behind his back and leaned forward, almost touching the back of the man.

Still, the man showed no sign of acknowledging David's presence.

Mara and Naomi had walked back to the stairs and sat on the bottom step, folding their dresses behind their legs, their eyes fixed on the man, then Eli.

Eli placed his hand on his hips.

David leaned forward more, his head now over the plane of the table's edge.

The man looked down, then to his right. He set the stone onto the black cloth and placed his hand atop David's head, ruffling his thick hair.

He set down the magnifying instrument, picked up David by the waist, and set him on his right knee.

"You have papers for me, Eli?" the man asked.

Eli stepped forward and set them on the table.

"And where are the girls?"

"Jessica is at home with Ruth, and the others . . ."

The man turned, looking over his shoulder, seeing Naomi and Mara on the steps, not budging, eyes wide, holding one another's hands.

His gaze darted from the twins to William. And fixed on William.

The face was older. The beard was whiter and shorter than when they had first met. The man was much thinner also, and if it were possible, he looked more robust and stronger than when William attended the game with him and Sir Thomas during the '05 Series.

The man lowered his head, raised David from his knee, and set him on the ground.

"I am sorry of Sir Thomas," he said to William. "He was a good friend. A good man."

On their walk home, Eli asked William, "Why didn't you tell me you had met Uncle Nathan?"

"I didn't know it was the same person. He frightened me. He doesn't talk much. I remember being nervous, so nervous at the game, I couldn't stop talking, rambling about all the players on the Athletics and Giants. I understand why the girls are scared of him."

Eli brushed his hand through the air. "Listen," he said to William. "None of us know Uncle too well. Don't think Mama even understands him. He doesn't fit anywhere. He's a rabbi but can't lead a synagogue because of his unorthodox lifestyle. He loves to study but gets restless. Goes west, away from the city, but always comes back 'cause this is his home."

***

Later that month, on a Sunday afternoon in late September, expecting to have an enjoyable meal, William arrived at the

Chalmerses' home and smelled none of the enticing aromas he usually noticed. Instead, Mrs. Chalmers opened the door and directed him to sit on a chair in front of the sofa. Seated there were the twins, Eli with Jessica on his lap, David, and Ruth. On another chair to the left of the sofa was Uncle Nathan. Mrs. Chalmers walked to the other end, opposite Nathan.

"We need your assistance, William," she said as she sat on the arm of the sofa, next to the twins. "The children have appreciated the games you have taken them. They, like their father, have grown fond of the sport. Uncle Nathan tells me that the leading teams in both leagues are so far ahead that it's a certainty the championship will be played in Chicago and Philadelphia. Is this correct?"

William was digesting the words and did not answer immediately, uncertain that he heard everything correctly or understood the intent with which the words were spoken, mostly because he was surprised to hear Mrs. Chalmers speak so knowledgeably about a subject he had previously thought she disdained, or at best, held to no value.

"Ahh . . . yes, this is correct . . . Cubs are way ahead in the National League . . . the Athletics in the American."

"Very well," Mrs. Chalmers continued. "As the Master of the universe ordained, there is a series of meetings we wish to attend in Chicago. They are scheduled to begin when the games will be played there. David and the girls will attend the meetings with me in Chicago, but we would all like to attend the games in Philadelphia. Would you be able to ensure that we could secure tickets?"

Uncertain he heard correctly, he looked to Eli.

Eli smiled, then shrugged.

He felt the whole pending arrangement suggested by Mrs. Chalmers was absurd. The entire family traveling westward, for baseball and whatever else beckoned them to Chicago, and for the matron of the family to place some responsibility of the journey into the hands of a thirteen-year-old kid, didn't make much sense.

"Ahh . . . yes," he said. "How many tickets is that?"

"Ruth is staying here with Jessica," Mrs. Chalmers answered. "That makes seven total in Philadelphia. The twins, David, Eli, Nathaniel, and myself. Plus you, of course. In Chicago, it will be just you, Eli, and Uncle Nathan."

But William started calculating other scenarios. If it were possible to get the seven tickets for Philadelphia from McGraw, couldn't it be just as possible to secure six for the games in Chicago so that Merlin and his parents could attend?

"Of course," Mrs. Chalmers continued, "we will pay for all the games and other expenses."

***

The games in Philadelphia were a delight.

Mrs. Chalmers, if it were possible, grew to be more beautiful than William had ever seen her. She was a different person away from the home. She seemed to transform from the children's mother to an older sister. Somewhere on the train between New York and Philadelphia, the twins left their window seat next to Eli and crossed the aisle to watch William defeat their uncle in checkers. Soon, the girls were playing, laughing with William and Uncle Nathan. By the time the train pulled into Philadelphia, the girls were asleep, Naomi with her head resting on Uncle Nate's left shoulder and Mara pressed against her on the other side.

Game one started late by about fifteen minutes as the captains of both teams discussed the ground rules with the four umpires.

"Four umpires?" William said with scorn to Eli and Uncle Nathan. "They've done fine with two in previous years. I guess the purpose of adding two umpires is to cause more hot air and delay the start of games!"

It wasn't much of a contest. The Athletics took an early two-run lead in the second and held on to defeat the Cubs, 4–1. Uncle Nathan seemed to enjoy the game. He was sitting on the edge of his seat, studying Chief Bender as he mystified the Cubs hitters.

The second game in Philadelphia was a carnival on the bases, at least for the Athletics. Although they were down early by one run in the first, they went ahead in the fifth, then scored six runs in the bottom half of the seventh, hitting two singles and three doubles.

They left Philadelphia on Tuesday evening and checked into their hotel in Chicago on Wednesday afternoon. While Mrs. Chalmers and the kids attended the opening gathering of an evangelistic crusade simultaneously occurring in different parts of the city, and while Uncle Nathan tracked down a friend of his with whom he served on Roosevelt's Rough Riders, William took the elevated train to Merlin's neighborhood to play several games of streetball.

On Thursday morning the girls and David had already left for a morning meeting at one of the Baptist churches. Eli, Uncle Nathan, and William walked to the West Side Grounds where they were to meet Merlin and his parents.

It took some convincing, but Merlin's father decided to forgo the profits of peanut sales so that he could attend the game. As the six of them approached the main gate, two policemen stopped them.

"They cannot enter," one of the officers announced, pointing at Merlin's father and mother.

"But they're with us . . . we've come before . . ." William said, pointing at Merlin.

"That may be," the other office said, "but not today."

William dug into his pants and held up the tickets. "But we have seats!"

"No matter. No coloreds."

Uncle Nathan reached into his coat pocket and opened his billfold. He whispered so softly that William could only hear isolated words: " . . . former New York officer . . . like you . . . under Theodore Roosevelt . . . served with him in Cuba . . . see, here are the papers . . ."

But none of this impressed the officers.

A crowd had gathered as Uncle Nathan shouted and pointed his finger at the policemen. One officer had removed the cuffs from his side and was about to corral Uncle Nathan's hands when William heard a familiar voice shout from behind. "What's all this, then?"

William turned to see BJ approaching.

"Mr. Johnson, sir," one of the officers explained, "we were explaining that we cannot allow this kind to enter the field—"

"And to what kind are you referring?" BJ asked. He placed his right hand on William's shoulder. "They are guests of mine."

BJ placed his left hand on the shoulder of Merlin's father. "This way, sir," he instructed, and led him to the turnstiles.

"Tomorrow, Mr. Jennings," he told William after they entered the park, "we meet at the same time, same location. There will be no issues. Yes?"

"Thank you, sir!"

Uncle Nathan and Mr. Jones shook BJ's hand. BJ tipped his hat to Mrs. Jones. Merlin raced up to BJ and asked, "Mr. Johnson, do you know Rube Foster?"

"Young lad," BJ said, "I will tell you something. Mr. Foster is a fine pitcher. Next to Matty, probably the finest I've ever seen."

The Athletics pitcher, Jack Coombs, did not pitch well, surrendering four runs, but all three Cubs pitchers pitched horribly, surrendering one run in the first, two in the second, five in the third, and another four in the seventh. The final score was 12–4, and the Athletics were one win away from sweeping the Cubs.

Torrential rains brought a reprieve for the Cubs, canceling the game on Friday afternoon. William had asked Eli whether he would like to spend the day with him and Merlin, but he chose to attend the meetings with his mother and siblings while Uncle Nathan escorted William and Merlin to Lincoln Park, the site of the World's Fair twenty years earlier. He treated them to breakfast and lunch, then met Merlin's parents for dinner. William and Uncle Nathan arrived back at the Hotel La Salle after nine o'clock.

Uncle Nathan opened the door of the room. On all previous occasions, Uncle Nathan held the door open for everybody. But on this evening, after taking a step back and making room for William to enter, Uncle Nathan turned his head with a surprised expression, seeing that the lights of the room had not been darkened.

"What's this, then?" he said, entering ahead of William. "Are the children ill?"

David and the twins were on the bed furthest from the door, each sitting up on their knees, eyes focused on their mother and Eli on the other bed. The bedspread on the children's bed had been removed and the sheets were disheveled, signs that the children at some point had been tucked in. The other bed was still unturned.

Eli was sitting up, his back propped against the headboard, with his mother to his right. Her left arm pulled Eli close so that his head rested on her shoulder. His face was red, wet, and swollen. His eyes released streams of tears.

"There is no use, Mama," he muttered through his sobs. "It will never change."

Mrs. Chalmers patted the side of Eli's face, as though he were a child waking from a nightmare.

"Five years ago it was no different," Eli continued. "It's the same now . . . just as it was then."

Uncle Nathan shut the door, walked to one of the two chairs in the room, and sat down across from the bed on which David and his sisters sat. He motioned for William to enter and to sit on the bed with the children.

Eli continued, his head lowered, his arm making frequent swipes under his nose. "You tell me what I already know. Papa told me what I already know. All the preachers we hear today—the Baptist, the Methodist, the Presbyterian—what they say . . . Mama . . . I know it!" Eli shouted, poking his index finger into his head, jabbing it as if he were attempting to drill a hole. "I know it, Mama!"

William shifted his eyes to David, hoping for some enlightenment as to what had brought this change in Eli's behavior.

"He'll be okay," David whispered, as if he knew what William wanted to ask.

"Mama will make it better," Naomi added, "though it hasn't been this bad since Papa."

Mara squeezed Naomi's hand. "Papa would always make it better," she said quietly.

Eli looked up at William. William saw in his expression a plea for help and shame for the blubbering fool he had become. Yet, the corner of Eli's mouth raised, as if he was glad of William's presence in the room.

"I am sorry, William," he said, wiping tears and sweeping his shirt sleeve beneath his nose. "I apologize to you and Merlin and his parents."

William looked to Uncle Nathan. He looked to Mrs. Chalmers, then to David, Mara, Naomi, desperate for some explanation as to what all this meant.

"I hated them, William," Eli announced. "I absolutely hated them. Yesterday at the gates, before Mr. Johnson escorted us into the stadium, I hated them for keeping us from getting inside, for making us the center of attention . . . for almost getting Uncle Nathan arrested . . . all because of them . . ."

Mrs. Chalmers reached out for Eli, but he pushed her away.

"All game long," he said, "I wanted nothing to do with any of them. Not Merlin or his mother or father. I hated Uncle for speaking with Mr. Jones so kindly. I hated you for being a friend with Merlin. Last night I went to sleep angry . . . hating all of them, hating all of you. I went to the meetings today, not because I wanted to hear a bunch of stupid, self-righteous preachers. I went to the stupid meetings today because I didn't want to spend any time with Merlin . . ."

Strangely, Eli did not seem as crazed as he had minutes earlier. He sat on the edge of the bed, swiped his sleeve again under his nose, and continued. "At the noon meeting, at the Southern Baptist meeting, a young Black pastor spoke of all that the Black folks endure in the South. 'Am I an idiot?' I asked myself as he continued to talk. 'Don't I see that the events we experienced outside the gates of West Side Park made me uncomfortable . . . made me angry?' It must feel a thousand times worse for Merlin and his parents."

Eli stood, untucked his shirt, and raised it to his nose. Before he had a chance to blow, Mrs. Chalmers reached up and pulled his right hand away from his nose and placed a clean handkerchief in his left. William wondered why she hadn't done this sooner.

Eli looked at the handkerchief, then at his shirt.

He placed the handkerchief in his pocket and raised the shirt back to his nose and blew.

"By the time we arrived here, I had all day to replay the hatred I felt for Merlin and all Black folks. How could I allow myself to feel such hatred? Why do I let such evil control me? Why is it so easy to give in to it all?"

At this point Eli dropped back onto the bed and buried his head in his hands. William could see the tears seep between Eli's fingers and his body begin to convulse.

"I understand," he screamed. "I understand your grace, yet I keep letting you down. I am so sorry . . ."

Mrs. Chalmers looked desperate, her eyes pleading across the room at Uncle Nathan.

But Uncle Nate was looking at the floor. He appeared in deep thought.

Minutes passed. Eli brushed away each of his mother's attempts at comfort.

"I'm hopeless," he grunted. "It's hopeless."

Uncle Nathan stood. "Let's go," he announced. "You." He pointed at Eli.

"You," and he pointed at William.

Eli looked at William. William looked at Eli.

"Now!" Uncle Nathan shouted as he opened the door.

They followed him out into the hallway, down the stairs, and onto La Salle Street.

They walked to a pub.

Uncle Nathan ordered a vodka for himself and sarsaparilla for the boys.

"Ice cream in both," he instructed the barkeep.

William had never had ice cream in soda and was anxious to discover how it might taste.

He would wait until Eli dipped his spoon into the concoction, not wanting to find enjoyment in this evening that had been a nightmare for his friend.

Uncle Nathan did not speak to either of them. He drank his glass of vodka, then ordered another.

Eli had yet to taste the soda and ice cream.

Once Uncle Nathan took a sip from his second drink, Eli spooned some ice cream and placed it on the tip of his tongue. Seconds later, he spooned another. He sipped through the straw, and this seemed to please him. He began alternating scoops and sips.

Within five minutes Eli and William had finished their treats.

Uncle Nathan went to the bar, returning with his third vodka. Behind him, the barkeep held two more sarsaparillas with ice cream, placing one before Eli and one before William.

When they returned to the hotel room, the room was dark, the children were asleep, and Mrs. Chalmers waited in the chair near the window.

Eli folded down the bedspread and sheets, rested his head on the pillow, and patted the pillow next to him twice, eyeing

William, inviting him to use the other side of the bed. William saw that Mrs. Chalmers wanted to speak with Uncle Nathan, but he immediately turned and closed the door. William could hear his footsteps descend the stairs. Maybe to get another vodka.

Mrs. Chalmers folded her arms across her chest and closed her eyes.

***

When William woke, Eli was cleaned, sitting on the edge of the bed, and looking anxious, but not with the look of internal turmoil William witnessed the previous evening. On the way to the game they did not speak, and as BJ led them through the main gates of West Side Park, Eli still had not spoken.

The game up until the third inning was boring. William was learning to love Connie Mack's "Mackies," or "Mackmen," as the Athletics were often referred to by sportswriters. They had scored twenty-one runs in the past two games, and William was anticipating more circus-type excitement on the bases. The young second baseman, Eddie Collins, was the catalyst—it seemed he was in the midst of all the scoring rallies. If the Mackmen needed a run, Collins was involved. And if Collins was the table-setter, Baker was the one Mr. Mack could rely on to score the men on base.

In the top of the third, the first pitch from Chicago's rookie hurler, King Cole, was a fastball that sailed over the head of the Athletics young shortstop, Jack Barry, not even close to the strike zone. The next pitch was a curve over the middle of the plate, but Barry did not swing, apparently thinking it was too low, and the plate umpire, Connolly, agreed, making the count 2–0. Cole threw another curve and Barry swung a bit early, hitting a high, lazy fly ball just behind third base and in foul territory, which Harry Steinfeldt could not run down. Pitch number four was a curve, and Barry hit this one much harder but still too early. It was a line drive over the head of Steinfeldt but clearly foul. Cole's next pitch was a fastball, and again, Barry hit this one on the sweet part of the bat, sending it further and higher than the previous pitch. But again, it was foul.

William inched to the edge of his seat. He looked around. A hush had emerged from the raucous cheering. Fans who had been screaming seconds earlier still applauded, but their cheering was more tempered. William recalled Sir Thomas telling him that the most exciting moments in a ball game are a triple, a hit-and-run, a double play, and a very long at bat. It had only been five pitches, but it seemed everyone in the stands felt the growing tension. Even Eli was sitting on the edge of his seat, and William heard him mutter, "C'mon Barry. You can do it."

Pitch six was a curve. Barry fouled it off the screen behind home plate, keeping the count 2–2. Pitch seven was a fastball inside, making the count full. Pitch eight was another fastball. Barry hit it harder than any of the other balls, sending it over the seats in left field—another foul. Cole's next pitch was a curve, and Barry fouled this one into the seats. Pitch ten was another curve, and Barry pulled this one on the ground straight to Steinfeldt, who cleanly fielded and threw Barry out at first.

Cole won the battle. Even got the next batter, Ira Thomas, to hit a lazy grounder to the mound for the second out. But he walked Chief Bender, then surrendered a triple to Amos Strunk, scoring Bender and tying the game. In the fourth the Athletics scored another two, taking the lead. Cole settled down in the late innings as his teammates rallied in the ninth to tie the score, then rallied in the bottom of the tenth to defeat the Athletics, 4-3, and earn their first victory of the Series.

Barry's long at bat enabled his teammates to see more of Cole's pitches as well as tire him: that is what Sir Thomas would have contended. But what was of even greater importance, Barry's at bat spoke to Eli—at least, that is what William concluded. After the inning ended, after the Athletics had tied the score, Eli stood, tapped William on the shoulder, and asked if they could switch seats.

"So," Eli said as he sat next to Merlin. "Have you ever seen Mr. Foster pitch?"

On Sunday the Athletics humiliated the Cubs, trouncing them, 7–2. The Athletics had won their first world championship.

Eli insisted that he sit next to Merlin at the game on Sunday. They continued speaking of Rube Foster and John Henry Lloyd and Pete Hill. They spoke of John McGraw and Frank Chance and Honus Wagner.

On Sunday, after the Series ended, Merlin and his parents boarded the elevated train. Eli hugged Merlin and thanked him for being such a good friend to William. He wrote his name and address on a piece of paper and handed it to him.

As the train traveled north into the horizon, Eli swiped the clean sleeve of his jacket under his nose.

1911

I t was the low barometric pressure along the Atlantic coast in combination with the low pressure over the Great Lakes that was causing the long delay of the 1911 World Series. At least this was the explanation William read in the *Philadelphia Inquirer* and *New York Times*. Connie Mack's Athletics had repeated as American League champs, and McGraw's Giants had fairly easily won the National League, moving into first place in late August, never relinquishing their lead, winning by a comfortable seven-and-a-half games.

At eight o'clock Saturday morning on the 14th of October, William arrived at the Polo Grounds long before the two o'clock start of game one. He had barely slept and received permission from his manager at the Newsboys Home to take the day off from selling papers. When he arrived at the clubhouse, the new uniforms had already arrived, just as McGraw had promised. They were in a large box in the center of the clubhouse floor. It was William's responsibility to place each player's uniform on the nail in their locker, along with the new cap. The jet-black uniforms were just like the uniforms William remembered from the '05 Series. He was certain of McGraw's intent: a sure reminder to Mack's team of their loss to the Giants six years earlier.

Although there had been a light October haze, the sun was out and the weather was comfortable. Matty and Chief Bender squared off in a low-scoring duel. Though it was not a shutout, Mathewson won again, just like six years earlier, beating Bender and the Athletics, 2–1.

The second game was scheduled for Monday, to be played at Shibe Park in Philadelphia. It rained most of Sunday, and although the sun was shining brightly Monday morning, there were still pools of water in Shibe's outfield, and the infield was more mud than dirt. Nonetheless, they played the game. The Giants young pitcher, Rube Marquad, held the lead, limiting the Athletics to one run and two hits through the first five innings. After the first two batters were retired in the sixth, Eddie Collins, the number three hitter, hit a ringing double down the left field line, sending up Frank Baker. The Athletics cleanup man had two clean singles off Matty in the first game, while Marquad had held him in check, striking him out in the first and causing him to hit a bounding grounder to Larry Doyle in the fourth. With Baker being one of the most feared hitters in the American League, William felt that limiting Baker to two singles was a contributing factor for the Giants' success.

Marquad's first pitch to Baker in the sixth was outside. Then he threw a biting curve, so deceptive that it started toward Baker's head, causing him to duck just as the ball dipped over the plate for a strike. In Baker's previous at bat, Marquad retired him on a high fastball over Baker's shoulders, at which he swung, causing him to hit the easy grounder to Doyle at second base.

Both Matty and Marquad had yet to pitch a fastball in the strike zone, mostly sticking to curves and junk pitches. For some reason, perhaps thinking he could outguess Baker, Marquad pitched a fast one into the zone, and the left-handed Baker made contact. The echoing crack of the ball getting beat up by the wooden bat in Baker's hands reminded William of the sound he regularly heard at St. Mary's whenever Brother Mathias hit fly balls to the boys or when George got ahold of a fat fastball, hitting it further and arcing it higher than any of the other boys on the Big Field could ever hope. Baker's ball sailed far over the right field wall, giving the Athletics a 3–1 lead. Eddie Plank shut down the Giants the rest of the game. The Series was tied at one.

The next day game three was back in New York. When Matty threw the first pitch in the first inning, there was a light drizzle. Through eight innings Matty was brilliant, giving up five hits, pitching a shutout. The Giants' run in their half of the third was the only run of the game. After retiring Collins in the top of the ninth, Matty's first pitch to Baker was a fadeaway for a called strike. His second pitch was a curve with a sharp break, at which Baker did not swing. It was called a ball by home plate umpire, Bill Brennan. The next pitch was another curve and low, also called a ball. Baker had yet to swing.

William studied Matty, wondering what wonderful musings were dancing inside his head. He had watched Matty play poker on the train with teammates and umpires and adoring fans. He had seen him play checkers, rarely losing to any challenger. William recalled the lessons taught by Sir Thomas regarding the guessing game between pitcher and batter, comparing it to the strategy in poker.

Whatever ingenuity was involved in the wit of baseball, Matty had more of it than most. The pages of T-reports in William's satchel and in the safe-deposit box at the Boys' Home were 70 percent Matty, 30 percent others. If William were to learn anything of value, anything that could be used in a game against an opponent, or anything that he could use if he ever played competitively, the lessons learned from observing Matty were sure to be of more use than what he learned from any other player.

Baker had not successfully made contact with any of the off-speed pitches thrown by either Matty or Marquad. William leaned forward, and he recognized Matty's stoic face. He figured the great pitcher was creating scenarios and theories based on what he determined Baker was expecting the next pitch to be.

Matty threw a fastball just off the inside of the plate.

Baker swung.

The sound was a crack that echoed through the park, louder and more damning than the sound William had heard the day before in Philadelphia.

The ball sailed into the right field bleachers.

The game was tied.

In the bottom of the tenth, Fred Snodgrass, the young Giants center fielder, earned a walk, stole second, and tried to advance on a high throw into center field, sliding hard into third base. William admired Snodgrass, mostly because he was from the southern coast of California and seemed to walk, play, and live with such ease that William dreamed of someday traveling west and lying on the beach, hoping to soak in the rays that might infuse him with the same qualities. As Snodgrass slid, he jumped with spikes high, knocking over Frank Baker and tumbling onto the infield dirt with him. He was called out, and even though it was Snodgrass's home crowd, William heard murmurings and fans shouting at Snodgrass that his play was dirty.

The Giants lost in the eleventh, 3–2.

The next game, in Philadelphia, was scheduled for Wednesday but was canceled because of heavy rain.

On Thursday it rained. The game was not played.

Meanwhile, the Philadelphia papers carried stories and editorials about the poor sportsmanship of Snodgrass. Athletics fans were lingering outside the Majestic Hotel, shouting threats. There was a rumor that somebody attempted to shoot him. There were other stories of the spikes causing blood poisoning in Baker's leg, hospitalizing him and making it questionable if the star of the Series would be available to play any more games.

On Friday it rained.

Though the rain was more of a mist, Shibe was a muddy mess. A story in the paper included a suggestion to drench the field with gasoline and set it aflame. William thought it a silly idea, likely originating from rabid fans desperate for play to resume.

Things continued to worsen for Snodgrass.

McGraw ordered him to return to New York until the Series continued.

On Saturday it rained.

McGraw surprised the team, allowing everyone to return to New York since no game would be played on Sunday regardless of the weather.

On Sunday there was no rain. There were no clouds. The sun was unhindered. Still, Shibe was in no condition for baseball.

All this rain, the low barometric pressure that experts claimed was causing the delay. William thought of how ridiculous it all was, how useless and hopeless and unfair and senseless the whole year had been. The delay of the Series was minor compared to the events occurring earlier that year. Events, William surmised, that may have found some relief had the barometric pressure in October traveled back in time and created all this moisture and rain in the spring.

From the edge of his bed at the Majestic, he had watched the rain fall for four days, listening to the patter as sheets of water paraded against the window. He had thought of how useful all this precipitation would have been during the early evening of March 25 back in New York. He had finished selling his last newspaper on Wall Street, then took the elevated train to Harlem, ate a quick lunch at the small café across from the Polo Grounds, and began making preparations in the clubhouse for the start of the Giants season opener. The team was in Marlin, Texas, enduring another heat-filled spring, McGraw's idea of preparing the team for the long season. "Spartan conditions", McGraw called it. Though the first game was still weeks away, this was William's fourth year, and he felt optimistic, wanting to make sure everything was perfect when the players arrived.

After completing his normal cleaning chores, he hiked up Coogan's Bluff, sat, and looked over the city. Below him at a steep vertical drop lay the Giants home field. To the east on the other side of the Harlem River was Hilltop Park, home of the Highlanders. He looked south, glancing over Central Park and onto Lady Liberty in the harbor. His attention was drawn to a gray cloud of smoke in the Lower East Side of the city. The cloud grew thicker and grayer, eventually becoming black. In the midst of the growing smoke, he saw flames reaching high into the sky.

***

"It was horrible," Ruth said, one week after the fire. For seven days she had stayed in her room, refusing to speak with any of her siblings, her mother, or Uncle Nathan.

"She has this look on her face," Eli had explained, "as if she woke from a nightmare, hoping to find someone to tell her that it was only a dream."

But William needed no description or explanation of Ruth's expression. He had seen it himself.

Upon seeing the smoke and recognizing that it was in the vicinity of the Chalmerses' home, he rushed down the bluff and raced to the nearest elevated train. Within an hour he was walking east on Orchard Street, relieved to see the fire behind him, still bellowing into the night sky but far from his friends' home.

Walking toward him was Ruth.

Her head was down, occasionally looking up at the flames, just as the crowd around her was. Her clothes were tattered and streaked with soot and dirt. The skin of her face was a mesh of ash and tears. She recognized William while he was still several feet from her, and for a brief moment the right side of the corner of her mouth rose. Then she rushed to him, fell to her knees, wrapped her arms around him, and wept.

Eli met William a week later outside of Pennsylvania Station while William sold his papers. "Ruth is more herself," he said. "Spoke this morning for the first time. Said she was hungry— could Ma fix her something? Wants to talk to us tonight, asked if you could join us."

This news made William happy. He felt guilty for feeling happy. Happy that Ruth had specifically asked for him to join the family.

How, he wondered, could something so tragic create within him a feeling of happiness?

From reading the papers he sold, he had learned the day after the fire that over one hundred employees, mostly young women and girls, had died in the fire that broke out at the building in which Ruth worked as a seamstress.

"Girls were leaping from windows," Ruth said at supper that night. She looked exhausted, her eyes downcast, her face pale, but William saw that her eyes no longer reflected the terror he saw one week earlier.

Ruth breathed in deep and shut her eyes, then continued. "I had been sent to the top floor to bring down the last shipment. All the girls were collecting their belongings, ready to go home. When I reached the tenth floor, I heard the alarm. There was panic, and I saw everyone rush to the windows, looking below. We could see the smoke rising. Girls had already broken the windows beneath us and were screaming to the people on the streets . . ."

Ruth stopped. She looked down at her plate, used her napkin to blow her nose, then gently pushed the plate away from her.

She nodded, as if to convince herself she could go on.

"I saw five girls leap from a window on the eighth floor . . . just as the fire engines began to arrive. When the ladders were fully extended, they only reached the seventh floor. They rescued as many girls as they could, but others began jumping—just stepped up on the sill and leaped—from the eighth and ninth floors. There was nothing to brace their falls . . . Maybe they thought the glass sidewalk coverings were strong enough to hold them, but they crashed right through them, falling onto the sidewalk, their bodies broken, like one of Mara's or Naomi's rag dolls."

William looked at the twins. Their eyes were fixed on their elder sister, each with one hand clutching a napkin, the other clasped to one another.

"We were helpless," Ruth continued. "We looked at one another, seeing the fate of those below, and we knew our moment was soon. The smoke was getting thicker, the flames were higher, and I could feel myself sweat. I began to imagine what it would feel like to be engulfed in flames . . . I thought of what all the girls below us had already endured and wondered what my choice would be . . .

"Then one of our supervisors shouted, 'Look!' We all turned to see where he was pointing. A group of young men on the building next to ours was on the roof, creating a bridge between our two buildings by placing large wooden boards and ladders, setting them on the ledge of their building. They waved for us to walk across. We rushed to the stairway and raced up to the roof. One of them was already on our roof and immediately directing us to cross, holding the boards steady as we shuffled from our building to theirs . . .

"We all crossed safely, and there was a pause as we looked at one another. Nobody spoke. Then more moments passed, and one by one we began to cry and hug the young men, law students from NYU. Eventually, the law students invited us to walk downstairs, but instinctively, I suppose, each of us walked to the edge of the building and looked down. Chaos all over—bodies sprinkling the sidewalk—girls leaping from the eighth and ninth floors. I saw a man kiss a woman, throw her from the window, then jump himself. A young girl I recognized was waving a handkerchief from a window on the eighth floor, desperate for someone to save her. She tried to jump to the university building, but her dress caught on a wire, and just as her hands stretched out to grab a ledge of a window, she fell to the pavement . . .

"I couldn't watch. I walked down to the top floor of the university, and some of the law students directed us to the elevator and escorted us out onto the street. The police had laid tarpaulins over the girls on the sidewalk. Firefighters were blasting all sides of the building with their hoses . . . Water was flowing down the building, like tiny waterfalls.

"I walked home. Ran into William just a couple blocks from the house. Seeing a familiar face that had nothing to do with the fire was such a relief—"

Ruth stopped and fixed her eyes on William. She smiled.

That smile melted something within William, and he felt a warm ember within his chest. As tragic as this had been for Ruth, the comfort William had brought to her, though he had done nothing heroic, made him feel as though he was special and important and that somehow he had something this family needed.

And the more he considered this, the angrier he became. The more bitter he grew toward the owners of the shirt factory. Newspaper articles appeared throughout the week, accounting the previous safety infractions that indicated negligence and greed by the men who profited from the girls' labor.

When the Giants' season opened on the 12th of April, just weeks after the fire, William invited Ruth and the rest of the family to come to the game, thinking that perhaps it might brighten her spirit and serve as a diversion. Between pitches, William glanced over to where Eli, Ruth, and their younger siblings sat just behind the Giants dugout. Ruth looked like the other sophisticated ladies William regularly saw in the grandstand, wearing a light-colored dress of lace, a flowered bonnet, and around her waist a ribbon belt that accentuated her hourglass figure. The twins wore simpler lace dresses and David was in knickers and wore one of William's old hats he had given him. Though the once-bright white had evolved into a faded yellow, the bold navy stitching of the letters *NY* was intact. And Eli was dressed like he was on his way to a job interview: pressed pants, vest, jacket with a collared shirt, snugly knotted tie, and a derby whose earth-toned features joined the sea of hats around it. Despite the Giants losing, 2–0, to the Phillies, William could tell they all enjoyed the game.

"Matty is pitching tomorrow," William told them after the loss. "He will certainly win."

And so they came again. Sat in the same seats. Matty did not pitch well, surrendering six runs. The Giants had lost the first two games of the season, being outscored 8–1. They were scheduled to play their next four games against the Dodgers. "They are sure to beat Brooklyn," he assured the family. "They are sure to put on a better show."

And though the family accepted his invitation, the game was canceled.

As William approached the park that morning, from a distance the Polo Grounds looked different. Something was missing. The outfield seats were no longer there.

He smelled smoke.

The stadium was surrounded by police and firemen.

Just after midnight, an officer a block away heard an explosion in the belly of the basement. By the time the fire engines arrived, the grandstands were destroyed. Only the left field bleachers and clubhouse were intact.

Two fires within three weeks. Earlier in the year, out in Los Angeles another explosion had killed employees at the *Times*

Building. Two brothers had been arrested and were currently on trial for this fire, the newspapers running daily stories of their alibis and attorneys and jury selection.

How was one to make sense of any of this mess? Fires, arson, death. The one-week delay of the World Series seemed meaningless in comparison to the tragedy in New York and the treachery in Los Angeles. The Giants had overcome the burning of the Polo Grounds to emerge as National League champs, assisted in part by the hospitality of the Highlanders owner in allowing the Giants to use Hilltop Park when the American League team was on the road. But what consolation was available for the victims in Los Angeles and the girls who jumped to their deaths or were charred in the fire at the Triangle Shirt Factory?

This question had been articulated by a new guest around the Chalmerses' supper table in late November, a month after the World Series had resumed and the Athletics defeated the Giants in six games, humiliating McGraw's team, beating them 13–2 in the final game. It was a tainted victory by Mack's team. William had caught the Giants opponents in the act of intercepting the signals Meyers was indicating for his pitchers. Between innings, after William had gathered the bats into the dugout and the Giants took the field, someone was signing to him from the stands. "Luther Taylor!" William exclaimed, spelling out with his fingers and smiling. "How are you?"

Luther did not answer, but immediately began to sign, instructing William to study the Athletics mascot and the third base coach, Harry Davis. After ten pitches, William discovered the urgency of Luther's message: the A's hunchback bat boy situated himself at an angle that enabled him to have a clear view of the signals Meyers was giving the pitchers. The boy was relaying the information to Harry Davis, who was then signing the next pitch to the batter. Is this why Baker hit those pitches from Marquad and Matty so far?

The discovery was too late. The Giants had lost. The city had one more thing to mourn along with the fires.

"Parts of suffering," the guest at the Chalmerses' home began, "I can understand—how it's caused by evil acts of other men like the brothers in Los Angeles. Or the owners' greed at Ruth's factory. But what of the innocent? Those who did nothing to warrant such pain and loss? Who simply were there living their lives, doing and being and contributing to what makes our society function?"

The guest spoke with a gentle voice and asked his questions as though he were not speaking to anyone around the table or did not expect answers. He seemed confused, troubled, anxious, frustrated.

William liked him. He understood why Ruth liked him.

The guest smiled at Ruth, and her eyes fluttered. She gently bit her lower lip, glanced down at her plate, and smiled.

"He's a law student," Eli had explained several days earlier to William, "one of the NYU students that helped Ruth escape the fire."

If William could be older, if he could be smarter, if he could be all that this young law student appeared to be, then he also might win over a lady as beautiful and kind as Ruth Chalmers.

"'Unless a grain of wheat falls into the earth and dies,'" the young law student continued, "'it remains alone. But if it dies, it bears much fruit.'"

"Jeshua?" Eli asked Jonathan, the young student.

"Yes," he answered, "but I quote him as Dostoyevsky does at the start of *Brothers Karamazov*, in hopes that perhaps, maybe, there is some point to the suffering we endure."

A voice spoke in barely more than a whisper from the far head of the table. William turned toward Uncle Nathan, surprised to hear him speak. At all the previous suppers at the Chalmerses' home, Uncle Nathan sat at the head and said the blessing, always addressing the giver of the meal as "Master of the universe," but then after finishing the prayer, saying little more. He lifted his head from his meal on occasion and appeared to listen intently to select conversations, but this was seldom. During most meals he focused his attention on the bread or the meat or the potatoes or some faraway place outside of the home, outside of the city.

"A rabbi," Uncle Nathan started, "many years ago, had asked the people a similar question—yes?"

Uncle Nathan raised his eyes.

Little David looked frightened. The twins giggled. Eli looked a bit lost. Ruth was smiling. Jonathan gazed at Nathan with what William surmised was respect, and Mrs. Chalmers did not look at Uncle Nathan at all. She had stopped eating and was staring at her place setting as if preparing for whatever words came next.

Uncle Nathan continued. "And as any good rabbi would do, his question was in response to a question he had been asked."

His voice was more audible now. He placed his hands on the table, folding his arms and setting one on the other. He closed his eyes and pressed them, as if trying to recite by memory.

"'There were present at that season some that told him of the Galilaeans, whose blood Pilate had mingled with their sacrifices. And the rabbi answering said unto them, "Suppose ye that these Galilaeans were sinners above all the Galilaeans, because they suffered such things?"'"

Uncle Nathan stopped and looked across the table at Mrs. Chalmers, then quickly turned and looked at Eli, then Ruth. But all remained silent as he continued.

"'Or those eighteen, upon whom the tower in Siloam fell, and slew them, think ye that they were sinners above all men that dwelt in Jerusalem?'"

Still, no one spoke. It seemed everyone was certain that he had more to say. The expressions around the table, however, had changed, and William was curious as to why all the children were staring at their uncle, their mouths and eyes wide in wonder. He surmised that the younger kids were confused, just as he, but Eli and Ruth were now mouthing words to one another in silence.

At the other end of the table, Mrs. Chalmers was still looking at her place setting. But William saw her glance up at her uncle and smile, her eyes sprinkled with tears.

***

Eli walked with William as he left the house to head back to the Newsboys dormitory.

They walked in silence for three blocks.

William sensed something was on Eli's mind.

"I'm leaving tomorrow," he announced.

William stopped and looked up at his friend. "Leaving?"

Eli nodded. "I spoke to Mama and Uncle. They say the kids will be fine. Now I need to hear from you."

"From me? I don't even know what you're talking about."

"I need to know you'll be okay. I need to know that I can trust you to write. Tell me how the kids are, the twins and their music, how David is doing at school. When Jesse speaks, is she still babbling nonsense, or is she making any sense? How's Mama holding up? Are Ruth and Jonathan getting serious? All of it."

"But . . . but—I don't even—where are you going? How long will you be gone?"

"Can you do it?"

William nodded. "How long will you be gone?"

"About two years," Eli answered. "It was only a week ago that a man from the Canal Zone gave a talk to our class. I couldn't pass up the opportunity. Leave tomorrow by train, down to New Orleans. Then catch a ship that will take me to Panama."

In the midst of a year of fires and rain delays and a loss to the Athletics, this news made William happy. Eli was leaving, escaping his home. He had never asked to be the man of the house, but he had no choice once his father died. It became his responsibility to care for the twins, and David, and Jessica. He cooked their meals, walked them to school, escorted them to the playground on the East Side. He was their protector while his elder sister and Mrs. Chalmers provided the resources. William sensed that Uncle Nathan was wealthy and assisted with expenses, but also sensed Mrs. Chalmers did not wish to abuse her uncle's generosity. Regardless, Eli would never embark on such a journey without the approval of his mother and uncle.

"All those stories Uncle Nathan told us while the kids played on the swings," Eli said as he looked up at the night sky, or maybe at the tops of the tall buildings; William could not tell. "The crews constructing the Brooklyn Bridge," Eli continued, mesmerized by whatever thoughts were dancing in his head, "men hanging from cables over the East River as they riveted beams—like watching a circus act. Week after week, month after month, year after year, until this monstrous architectural achievement could be seen exploding from our shore. And then it met an equally enormous structure in the middle of the river from the opposite shore. We cross a body of water that one could never have imagined could be crossed . . .

"And now, William, now I have a chance to do what those men on the construction crews did—be a part of something that will be remembered, seen, and used to benefit our generation and the next, and the generations long after us."

Thirty minutes earlier, Uncle Nathan and Jonathan were talking about things he hardly understood. But *this* he understood. The adventure upon which Eli was to embark made Eli happier than William had ever seen him. And though he was happy for Eli as he boarded the elevated train, looking out the window toward the street that led to the Chalmerses' home, he feared that despite Eli's words minutes earlier, the rest of the family may no longer welcome him as they did when Eli was amongst them.

1912

—∞—

Postmark: Canal Zone, Panama City, Panama

December 12, 1911

Hola William,

Feliz Navidad, mi amigo!

I just boarded the train in Ancon and will arrive at my "office" four to five miles westward in about 20 minutes. I write as heavy rain pelts the train's windows, the wind so strong that the water vibrates the glass as it hits, approaching, it seems, at a right angle to the window, parallel to the ground. It's not the type of rain we have in the city. It's a relentless rain, never stops, as if the clouds above are perpetually sad and they can't stop weeping. The air is heavy and thick and sticky. In a word, it's quite disgusting, but after the first two weeks I have acclimated to it, I think.

I apologize for not writing sooner. I got sick on the boat one day prior to arriving and was not able to begin work at the cut until a week later. But now I feel as though I am settling, making friends, learning, and contributing.

The home I share with other bachelors is quite comfortable, and I look forward each day to that moment when I am able to lay my head on the white cotton pillowcase. I never felt so appreciative of a night's rest as I do after a day's work here.

I wake at five, read by candlelight until the others awake, then we walk to the train. By seven we are working—digging, driving excavating shovels, loading dirt onto railway cars, placing ignitions in the next piece of rock that will be blasted, and all the other things that must be done to accomplish what we are striving to accomplish. By the time we get back to our barracks, usually around six, we eat supper and go to bed. The exhaustion I have felt is like nothing I have experienced before. I guess some of it has to do with the humidity, but for the most part it's a good exhaustion. What I mean is that I feel so satisfied each evening as I close my eyes, happy that I am so tired, happy that I have worked my body to limits I am able to keep pushing, happy that I am able to do it for this grand purpose. Unfortunately, all this translates into the fact that this is the first letter I have written.

Please tell me about the kids. How is Mama? Will you be able to celebrate the holidays with the family?

We've not spoken much about our friendship, William, but I think you know—I hope you realize that even if I've not said it, I want to write it. I want to write it clearly that you, William Jennings, are a good friend. You have helped me entertain the kids, you have accepted all our invitations to dinner, you were the first to comfort Ruth after that horrible fire, you listen and laugh and share in our family meals. You are a primary reason Mama and Uncle gave their blessings for my journey south.

Well, the rain has suddenly stopped. The sun is unhindered. The dark clouds that only minutes earlier were thick overhead I can now see scurrying away eastward, over the Atlantic.

It's off to work!

Write soon.

Your amigo,

Eli

Postmark: New York, NY

January 18, 1912

Dear Eli,

Your letter made my day not so horrible. Since celebrating Christmas (and Chanukah) with the children, your mother, and Uncle Nathan, I have been dragging, very sad. There seems to be nothing to look forward to, nothing to brighten this dark, cloudy, cold weather. The start of the season is still three months away, and my days begin like they have for the past three years: waking before dawn, grabbing a stack of papers, and dragging myself to Wall Street or Penn Station or Grand Central, hoping to return to the Home with no papers and many nickels.

Your mother purchased several presents for me, and the family watched while I opened each of them. Why, even the twins and David gave me a present. I looked up as I was untying the ribbon, and the three of them were wide-eyed, staring at me. I was frightened that perhaps whatever was underneath the wrapping might not be something I want, and my reaction, albeit unintentional, may be disappointing for the three of them. However, my fear was unwarranted. When I opened the lid of the box, inside was a book, a big book, leather bound, with bold gold leaf lettering on the cover. The pages were thin, but I suppose that's because there were so many. As I ran my hand across the fresh leather, feeling the bumps of the raised gold letters, I felt an exhilaration similar to the excitement I felt when Brother Thomas took me to those early World Series contests. I think I might have cried had David not started to clap and begun dancing. "You were right!" he shouted to Naomi and Mara. "He likes it!" I ran my fingers across the lettering again, first across the name of the author, Victor Hugo, then the title, *Les Miserables*. I had never dared to check it out from the library, fearful that I could never finish it by the due date. I began to lift it to my breast to hug it, but then thought I may look silly embracing a five-pound book like a child embraces a teddy bear, so I looked at the three of them, lowered my head as though I was bowing with gratitude, and told them softly, "Thank you."

The festivities at your home during the week of Chanukah and Christmas were filled with memories like this, which has made the days of January all the more dreary. Venturing to the library after I have sold the papers is the only thing I have to look forward to each day. The kids are busy at school. David has made new friends, so my friendship is no longer needed. The girls attend a music conservatory after their classes are finished, and your mother and Ruth are at work. Uncle Nathan picks up little Jesse in the morning and watches her while he works in his basement.

But this morning, outside of Penn Station, feeling especially down because I still had half the stack of papers I had carried from the Home, I saw Uncle Nathan walking toward me. And you know what? I think I may have smiled! He was dressed in his black robe, and though it was pressed and clean, I imagined it would not be by the end of the day, for he was with baby Jesse. She was at Uncle's left side, reaching up, holding his hand. The moment I saw them, all the commotion around the station excited her and she broke free from Uncle, racing from one vendor to the next, pointing, mumbling something that surely Uncle Nathan could not understand, and while he raced to catch up to her at one vendor, she scurried to another. He chased her from one side of the plaza to the steps leading to the station, then to the other side of the street. Finally, he scooped her into his arms and approached me as I was in the midst of a sale.

"Mr. Jennings," he said, "I see you still have many papers to sell. We will assist you."

He handed one paper to Jessica and pointed toward the center door leading to the trains. He must have discussed this with her earlier because she immediately obeyed, and within thirty seconds she returned with a nickel. He handed to her two more papers; she returned with two nickels in less than a minute. Then three papers— she struggled at first, dropping one onto the cool pavement, then stopped and dropped the other two, strewing the pages, making a disorganized mess of all three. But two businessmen dressed in fine suits bent to their knees, gathered the papers and organized them, and each handed Jesse a dime, keeping one paper and giving her back the other two. She was looking around, confused, and said something that sounded like "Thank you," turned back around to seek further instruction from Uncle, and bumped into a woman who handed her a dime with one hand and grabbed one of the two newspapers Jesse held with the other. By eight o'clock I was sold out.

"Are we done, then?" Uncle Nathan asked.

I said nothing. It seemed obvious I had nothing left to sell.

"Good," he said, turning, grabbing Jessica's hand. "Follow us."

"But I need to return to the Home," I explained, "turn my money in, balance the sales."

"Mr. Jennings," Uncle said, "when do they expect you to return?"

"Ten . . . ten thirty."

"We will have you back by then. This will not take long."

I could have asked where he was taking me, but I assumed he preferred I just follow him and Jesse. So, in their wake I walked.

We took the train to Wall Street and walked one block east to the steps of National City Bank. I recognized the building; I'd often sold papers across the street but had never ascended the steps, much less gone inside. My supervisor at the Home had taken a few of us to open accounts at one of the smaller banks near our residence, so being inside a bank was not new to me, but this—oh my! I imagined I had gone back in time, walking through Versailles on my way to meet Emperor Napoleon. The floors were marble, clean and shiny. Lights hung from the ceilings. Brass cages had important-looking men behind them wearing spectacles and counting bills handed to them by customers. Whenever I handed money to the people behind the cage at the East River Bank, it was always nickels and dimes, occasionally fifty-cent pieces, but here, at almost every window men and women were handing bills to the bank men. And at some windows the bank men were handing bills to the customers! Wouldn't that be something!

"This way," Uncle directed me in a soft voice, as though we were in a library.

He introduced me to the bank manager, but I can't remember his name. I was a bit overwhelmed. Why was your uncle introducing me to a man like this? The whole scenario was absurd. It made me feel like I also was important.

The bank manager walked us through a set of swinging doors, past the desks of employees busy punching numbers into machines, busy writing numbers on small pieces of paper, so busy that I did not notice any of them pay us any attention. Only once a lady looked up, smiling at little Jesse.

We reached a room in the back, and the manager directed the three of us into a small room with a curtain. A few moments later he returned with a box. He handed the metal box to Uncle Nathan, and Uncle set it on a little table in the room. He reached under his robe and took out a set of keys on a ring. The smallest key he placed inside the lock on the metal box and opened it.

"Now. Mr. Jennings," he began, "these are your belongings. Whatever is inside this box is your property. You understand?"

I nodded, though I did not. No, I definitely had no understanding as to how anything inside this box could possibly belong to me. Besides, all that was inside was a small brown-shaded envelope. I looked down at Jessica, and she was gazing up in delight at the three sparkling stones Uncle Nathan had just emptied from the envelope. The three stones were like pebbles of glass, and the faded light in the room danced through them. Little Jesse reached up, but Uncle placed them back inside the brown envelope.

"I have a key," Uncle said, pointing to the key on the ring, still protruding from the lock on the metal box, "and now you will have a key." He reached inside his robe and handed me a second key ring. But this key ring held only the one key.

"Here," he invited. "You try." Uncle placed the envelope back inside, closed the lid of the metal container, and removed his key from the lock. He held out his hand, inviting me to place the key he just gave me into the lock. I placed it inside. It fit smoothly into the crevice, and I turned it, hearing a clean *click* that filled me with happiness. Whatever all this meant, it seemed to be important, and I began to imagine, "If those three pebbles of glass belonged to me, what if they were diamonds? How much are they worth? And of even more importance, if these three pebbles are mine, how did they come into my possession? Who decided they belonged to me?"

"I'll explain it all later," Uncle said, interrupting all the thoughts dancing through my head. "I wanted to show these to you now, for one purpose. How they got here, why they belong to you, is not important. What is crucial is that you understand that the value of those stones is to be used for one purpose and one purpose alone—to fund your college education."

I nodded again but was even more confused, more mystified. I had spoken of college to nobody. I have not been inside a normal classroom since the day I left St. Mary's. What I have learned, I learned at the library or on the streets or at the ballpark or at the synagogue school I sat through while waiting for the kids to be dismissed. The thought may have passed through my brain once or twice, but the reality of who I am, the uncertainty of where I came from—how could I ever think that college would be possible? But here was Uncle Nathan, explaining a fact, that these stones would be used for no other purpose, as if he had no question in his mind that college was in my future.

Had you had any idea of any of this?

Write soon. I suspect by the time I receive your next letter, the season will have begun.

Sincerely,

William

Postmark: Canal Zone

February 29, 1912

Señor Jennings,

I have witnessed a little boy maturing into a young man.

When you arrived on our doorstep four years ago, we were strangers, and if it were not for Papa and Brother Thomas, we likely would have never met. Now you are faced with making decisions that likely will determine the path you travel the remainder of your days. Papa always said that building things made me the happiest, that I became the most excited when there was a new puzzle he brought home or when he and Uncle Nathan would take me to the shore of the East River to watch the crews' progress on the Williamsburg Bridge. This explains my attraction to engineering and what compelled me to journey to Panama. There are things that make you equally happy, I am sure, things that get your blood boiling, make you feel alive. I know baseball is one of those things, and perhaps you can find a way to make a living on the field. But in the meantime, Uncle is correct. You need to go to college. And regardless of the type of classroom in which you have been educated, I believe you are more qualified than any of the traditionally educated fourteen-year-olds to pursue a degree.

Although I still have two years to finish my degree, I have no regrets about coming down here. Early last fall, during what was supposed to be another structural engineering lecture by my professor at the university, one of the chief engineers working on the canal spoke to our class. He spoke of the progress that had been made in a ten-year span and of the history of the French work done twenty years earlier. He spoke of the likelihood that the work would be complete within the next three years, of the opportunity for each of us in the class to get hands-on experience, return to the States, finish our education, and with the work of the canal as part of our resumé, be set for life. Less than a month later, I was on the boat to Panama.

The men who have been here the longest told me of the dire conditions when they arrived. They describe all the progress that has been made. The greatest fear has always been disease—yellow fever and malaria. During the French effort, 20 percent of those who arrived died because of these two diseases. Another 20 percent got so sick that they were unable to work. In 1902 during the early stages of the US effort, before the "real" work even began, over two hundred had died. The scare was so potent that some of the potential workers arriving by ship, when hearing of the epidemic, immediately got back on board and went back to their homes. But a Dr. Gorgas changed all that. Somehow, he had all but ended malaria and yellow fever in Cuba two years earlier. Upon arriving in Panama he instituted what seemed to be bizarre remedies. Even today I see these bizarre solutions walking the streets—dark-skinned men from Jamaica and Barbados with large metal tanks strapped to their backs, stopping every few feet to spray a pool of water, a possible breeding ground for the larvae of mosquitos. In the tank is a mixture of oil and chloroform. Often, they bend over to fill vials with the stagnant water, I suppose to take it to Dr. Gorgas's staff and ensure that there is no lurking malaria outbreak. The end result is that disease amongst the workers has disappeared. There are deaths, yes, many deaths, but they are mostly due to accidents on the job.

It is progress such as the conquering of disease that fills me with gratitude and wonder. What has been accomplished down here over the past ten years surpasses the construction marvels of the bridges in our city. The nine miles of the cut are well over 50 percent complete. And I have the privilege of joining this wondrous effort.

May I humbly suggest to you, my friend, that you also seek to discover that skill which you possess so you also can join a great effort.

Your amigo,

Eli

Postmark: New York, NY

August 29, 1912

Dear Eli,

I feel I have let you down. It was exactly six months ago you wrote, and I've not received any other letters from you. I am hoping that you are not too angry at me. What's more, I fear I have failed to protect the kids in your absence. Naomi and Mara are in good hands. Once classes ended in early June, they boarded a train with Uncle Nathan, traveling west to Kentucky. One of Uncle's fellow Rough Riders settled there and holds music camps for kids across the country. They are supposed to return next week.

With Uncle gone, Ruth and your mother have juggled taking care of little Jesse. I've tried to help when I can, but McGraw asked me early in the season to travel with the team on most of the road trips. He has asked me to keep files of T-reports on some of the key players on the other teams. I don't think he's used any of my observations during a game, but he often makes suggestions to improve my reports and explains why players have certain habits, even when they know it is detrimental to their performance on the field. He said it is in our nature to be obstinate, to not want to take another's advice. He tells me the most coachable players tend to be those who have attended college—not because they are smarter than the others on the team, but because they value learning and are more keenly aware of their own weaknesses, more eager for others to suggest how they can improve.

Once, while we were traveling to Pittsburgh, as the rest of the team was sleeping, he beckoned me over to discuss Honus Wagner. There wasn't much to discuss regarding strategy. Most of what he told me was in praise of the stocky shortstop, that the best way to pitch him is to throw it over the plate, hoping that he hits it on the nose and it goes straight to one of the fielders. Trying to outguess him or to dance the ball to quadrants of the plate he is less likely to reach is pointless. His hand-eye coordination is the best in the game, and his arms are like an octopus, reaching all parts of the strike zone. Eventually, McGraw stopped talking and flipped through more pages of my notes. I shut my eyes, but before I fell asleep, I quickly opened them, just in time to see McGraw reach inside his inner jacket pocket, taking out a small black book. He jerked his head toward me, and I shut my eyes, feeling that he did not want me to know of the book. Naturally, my curiosity heightened, and for the next ten minutes I stole glances of him turning pages, writing notes, staring up at the car's ceiling, looking out the window at the passing darkness. He held the book close to his chest, looking over his shoulder, writing more notes, staring into more nothingness.

As I had been traveling with the team, I began to notice this occur with more frequency, perhaps only because I had caught him in the act and was determined to discover what was contained inside the little book. I didn't dare ask; I think he would have erupted into one of his cursing episodes and likely would have rid me of my position. Though I never saw the words inside the book, I did notice a pattern emerge. Whatever he wrote in the book, the looks on his face became more longing and the pen struck the page with greater intensity on those days we visited cities like Chicago, Philadelphia, and Pittsburgh, cities in which some of the more prominent teams from the Negro leagues reside. These teams often play doubleheaders, so McGraw would leave the hotel early to catch the first game. I first discovered this in Chicago at a game I attended with Merlin. There was Little Napoleon in the front row, wearing his straw hat, dressed in his finest suit. Was it the style of play that tortured his imagination? Was it the quality of play that he witnessed? Was it the players he coveted?

We had just returned from a long road trip and were at home for a short two-game home stand against Brooklyn. That afternoon when I was returning to the clubhouse after getting a quick bite to eat, most of the players were there playing cards and checkers or reading the newspaper. As I passed each of them, without exception they looked up at me, smiling the kind of smile that means they know something that I don't. I began to fear that McGraw knew I had seen him and his little black book. I feared that this was my last day in the clubhouse. But if none of the players knew of the book's existence, why would they be smiling?

And my anxiety heightened when I spotted in the corner of the clubhouse the odd-looking, tall, lanky team mascot, Charlie Faust. He was still dressed in his street clothes—his black suit and black derby hat. He had just taken the hat from his head and held it between his hands, dancing his fingers on the brim, looking directly at me and smiling as if he also was aware of whatever the joke amongst the team might be. Normally, the humor in a situation escaped him. Typically, he was the humor of a situation and was not aware that others found him amusing. Last season he showed up one day in St. Louis, Fred Snodgrass explained to me, approached McGraw in a hotel, and insisted on being given a tryout, convinced that his presence on the team would ensure the Giants' winning the pennant. This assurance was based on a consultation he had with a fortune-teller who told him, "You will be a great pitcher." McGraw saw that the man was serious and played along, I guess thinking it may help the team forget the bad rut they had fallen into. He gave the tryout, letting the man pitch, take batting practice, and run the bases, and the team loved him. They laughed when McGraw removed his catcher's mitt to catch the pitches from the strange man, laughed when the team fumbled the weak grounders he hit to them, allowing him to round the bases. What they didn't laugh at was when the team's fortunes changed, when we swept the Cardinals that road trip, when he showed up at the Polo Grounds later that year and we started winning with regularity. They didn't laugh when the team lost three games straight after Mugsy's attempt to rid the team of the nuisance of Mr. Faust by securing a vaudeville contract for him, nor did they laugh when Faust returned and we won eighteen out of twenty-two on the next road trip. Even Hank O'Day, the grumpy umpire, would jump cars on the train to come witness the antics of Faust. And when we lost the Series last year, amidst all the scandalous accusations about sign stealing, McGraw sent Faust to pick a fight with the A's mascot. All this to say, when I saw Mr. Faust—this man who never seemed to be aware of the humor around him—smiling and amused at me, I feared something horrible awaited.

As I passed Matty, he told me, "McGraw wants to see you in his office."

I looked over my shoulder, and all the players were standing. Larry Doyle placed two fingers in his mouth and let out a high-pitched whistle. Meyers began to holler. Marquad started clapping. Even the young rookie, Jeff Tesreau, let out a deafening shout. "Yoo-hoo!"

I looked at Matty, hoping he would offer some explanation. He motioned to the door and said, "Pretty lady."

I walked to McGraw's office, knocked, then turned the knob. Upon opening the door I saw the back of a flowered bonnet that looked familiar. The woman sitting in one of the three chairs opposite McGraw turned. It was your mother.

"Hello, William," she said, as McGraw stood and motioned for me to sit in one of the other chairs.

"Have a seat, Mr. Jennings," he said, addressing me with an air of dignity I did not recognize. Even the fact that he addressed me as Mr. Jennings was a bit of a shock. Usually it was "Hey, you," or "Boy," or "Jenny," or at best, "Willy."

McGraw waited for me to sit, cleared his throat, then told me, "Mrs. Chalmers speaks very highly of you."

He paused.

I felt I ought to look over at your mother and offer some sign of gratitude, but I was shaking and sweating. I was not comfortable. Here I was in McGraw's office, sitting next to your mother, one who has welcomed me into her home and shown me kindness, and across from us was the man I feared daily—feared to disappoint, feared to cross the bats of the players and jinx their offensive prowess, feared overstepping my sense of importance as we studied together the T-reports of the opposing team, feared witnessing one of his many tirades during a game such as an argument with an umpire or cursing or taunting the other team.

Why was your mother here?

McGraw continued. "Mrs. Chalmers tells me you are bright. To be honest, I had known this already, and forgive me that I did not say this sooner, Jenny, but for a boy your age, you are perhaps the lad who has impressed me the most of any boy we've had on the team. Your insights on those reports compete with some of the men we pay for such efforts."

I felt he was talking about someone other than myself. Never had he spoken any words like this. He went on for a while longer, and I was getting very uncomfortable. Then I heard him say the words, "You will no longer travel with us on the road this season."

I looked up at him, fearful of the whole black book scenario.

"You will attend the school Mrs. Chalmers's children attend. You will finish the school year so that you have an academic record. Something that will help you gain admission to a college of your choice."

This is why he called me into his office? This is why your mother was here? First, it was Uncle taking me to the bank, making sure I understood that I could afford college. Then you invested most of your last letter in persuading me of the value of an education. Now your mother and Little Napoleon!

After your mother left, McGraw asked me to stay seated. He proceeded to instruct me that my last road trip of the year would be in two days, when we depart for a three-game series against the Braves. While the rest of the team would depart from Boston for seven games in Philadelphia, I would remain in the city. "Do what you like there, Jenny," McGraw told me. "No finer city to be educated in than Boston."

Immediately, I stopped wondering about college. I heard nothing of what McGraw might be saying. He was still speaking, but upon hearing that I would be left in Boston and that the team was leaving on the 3rd of September, my thoughts raced. I was keenly aware of the pending matchup on September 6 at the newest ballpark in the American League, across town at the Fenway. There, the flamethrowing Walter Johnson of the Senators would be pitching against Boston's hard-throwing Smoky Joe Wood. If the standings remained, we would likely see the Sox in the Series.

McGraw was snapping his fingers, waking me from my trance.

"And," McGraw continued, "I want you to stay in the city, go to Fenway, watch Wood throw. I want a detailed report on him. Understand?"

Dear Mr. Eli, dear Uncle Nathan, Mrs. C., and the entire Chalmers family—and yes, I will say it, dear Mugsy McGraw— what does all this mean? Can it be possible? I'm a newsboy, a rugrat.

College?

Really?

Hope you are well.

William

Postmark: Canal Zone

September 10, 1912

William,

Life is ugly. You know this. I know this. All of us down here in the Zone witness new manifestations of this on a daily basis.

In the cut, amid the rain and humidity, the deafening combination of mammoth steam shovels digging, rock drills boring, and dynamite blowing in a distant canyon all combine to form an eerie orchestration. It may sound like chaos, but really, it's all a by-product of men working toward a common goal.

Let me tell you what a typical day of mine is like.

Upon arriving at Culebra, I report to the engineering hut and learn whether any mudslides occurred overnight. Now, let me tell you 'bout the slides. About half the work the French did in the 1880s turned out to be useless, mostly because of the slides that occurred after they left. It wasn't as though the French didn't experience slides while they were working on the cut. They did, and the slides' intensity seems to increase with each sign of progress we make. At times it seems pointless, working months and years on the nine-mile cut only for slides to occur at various spots, creating a disruption, causing us to invest our efforts in cleanup that might last two to three months before cutting can resume.

We make efforts to prevent the slides, making small canals parallel to the cut to trap water, minimizing (hopefully) the possibility of future slides, and we increase the angle of the cut, hoping that the steeper we cut, the less likely a slide will occur.

Unfortunately, this year has been futile. Already, at least a third of our time has been spent on cleanup.

I mentioned earlier the eeriness of the sounds in the canyon. Allow me to describe the eeriness of the mudslides. When I am present to witness a slide, it is often accompanied by cracks appearing in the rock and smoke issuing through the fissure, as if we have disturbed a sleeping volcano underneath. Then, as the mud moves down the sides of the canyon, the ground below begins to rise ten, fifteen, or even twenty feet into the air, like we are on a slow-rising elevator. I've had it explained to me by those who have been here the longest that it's like pressing on a clump of dough—rolling a lump at one spot causes another section of the dough to rise.

My job when these slides occur is to work with our team to rearrange the railroads throughout the cut. On a normal day our schedule is hectic, working timetables for the passenger trains in and out of Culebra, making sure the excavation cars filled with dirt and rock are not disrupted in their journey to the dumps one to twenty miles from the cut. As good progress is made, we are constantly recalculating the best location for the tracks. This requires us to move the tracks quickly, which we are able to do thanks to this thing called a trackshifter. It's kind of like a crane, but I don't completely understand how it works. Each time I see it in action, I stare in wonder at the twelve workers maneuvering the shifter to move the tracks to a new location. Prior to the shifter, it would take over 150 workers to move a section of track one mile. Now we are able to accomplish it with only the twelve.

But when a slide occurs, the routine is disrupted. Throw all our calculations out! Have to start from scratch.

I take solace, however, in the history of how we arrived at this day, in the assurance that despite the setbacks, Providence has favored us. Perhaps Master of universe favors our efforts, just as we believe he blessed the efforts of those who built the bridge, of those who sailed the globe, of the builders of all the great civilizations. Who knows? Am I rambling?

Still, prior to the start of the construction ten years ago, while Congress was determining the best site for the canal, most of our legislators favored a location north of Panama, in Nicaragua. It was just before a vote was taken that a series of volcanic eruptions occurred in Nicaragua, and tens of thousands died. After long debates, the Senate approved to move the canal site to Panama.

So, Mr. Jennings, despite the ugly events that occurred prior to your birth, and despite the ugly events that have occurred since your arrival on this planet, my advice is to keep the end in sight and look back every now and again to observe that from which you have come.

Adios.

Eli

Postmark: New York, NY

September 25, 1912

Dear Eli,

Wow!

Wow—wow—wow!

The pitching wonders that have been accomplished this season! By three hurlers in particular.

One is our own Rube Marquad. He started the first game of the season in Brooklyn, defeating the Robins, 18–3. It was a sign of things to come. On July 3, Marquad won his nineteenth game, an amazing 19–0! On July 8, he finally lost.

Meanwhile, in the American League, Walter Johnson had won sixteen consecutive starts, and by early September, Joe Wood of the Red Sox was in the midst of a thirteen-game win streak. On September 6, the day McGraw asked me to take notes on Wood, Boston's ace had a record of 29–4. Walter Johnson was 28–10. All the papers were headlining the matchup. Taft, Wilson, and Roosevelt would pay handsomely for such publicity! The nation was more concerned about the matchup at Fenway on an early fall afternoon than they were about the election two months away!

You used the word "eerie" a couple times in your last letter. I will use it here. Our season began in Brooklyn for a three-game set. Then we came to Boston for the next three games of the season. The players were down, having lost two games in Brooklyn to the lowly Robins. But upon arriving at the ballpark in Boston, we received the news of the *Titanic*'s sinking in the North Atlantic. Our 1–2 start didn't seem to matter much that day. I suppose that's why we lost to the hapless Braves, making our record 1–3. But from that point of the season forward, the season has been golden. We've been in first place since May 21, and here it is early September, and the closest team is eight back. It's very likely we'll be facing the Red Sox in October for the championship, thus McGraw's request for me to complete a T-report on Mr. Wood.

The crowd at Fenway was full of anticipation. The atmosphere was similar to a game in October. All the seats were filled, with thousands of fans crammed onto the outfield grass. Nine years ago I was in Boston with Brother Thomas for the first Series against Pittsburgh and recall the many fights and pushing, but there was none of that today. Everybody's attention was focused on the pending drama.

The Senators leadoff man started the game with a clean single just past Boston's third baseman, Larry Gardner. And though it was stopped by Boston's shortstop, by the time he fielded the ball, there was no point in throwing. The next batter hit a weak grounder to Wood, and he turned a double play. Then Wood struck out the next batter. Johnson also gave up a hit in the first, but after a fielder's choice and a caught stealing, both pitchers faced the minimum in the opening inning. Through five, the game was scoreless, both teams with just three hits each. Then in the bottom of the sixth, Tris Speaker went the other way, hitting a liner down the left field line for a clean double. Though there were already two out, the next batter, Duffy Lewis, hit him in despite the valiant effort of the Senators right fielder, diving and almost making a brilliant catch to stop Speaker from scoring. And that was it. The only run. Just about what was to be expected between these two greats. Johnson struck out five batters, and Wood struck out eight.

As for the three days between the Giants' departure for Philadelphia and the great matchup on the 6th, I visited the campus of Boston University, Boston College, Emerson, Tufts, Northeastern, and Harvard. What is the saying—saving the best for last? Such is my hope and dream. We will see.

Sincerely,

William

Postmark: Canal Zone

October 5, 1912

William,

You mentioned in a letter earlier this year about McGraw's little black book, perhaps not intending the irony of such alliteration. Based on your observations of the Giants skipper, it appears he bemoans the line that has been drawn in our nation, the line that does not allow the descendants of former slaves to participate on the same field of play with those who have lighter skin. The sport of baseball is not the only arena in which this line appears. Its presence is everywhere. I was reminded of this darkness within my soul when we visited Chicago together a couple years ago, and though this darkness has dispersed some, I still struggle with its remnants. Since it was unhindered to fester all those years prior, I imagine it will take some time to totally rid myself of its ugly face. The presence of this line is everywhere down here in Panama.

Of the thirty to forty thousand workers, most are from the islands in the Caribbean. There are only about five to six thousand that look like you and me. Most of the workers come from Barbados, some from Martinique, smaller numbers from the other islands. There are some from Jamaica, but I've been told that the Jamaican government levies a heavy tax on those who leave the country. They lost so many during the French effort twenty years ago that they felt this was the only way to stop another mass exodus. Most of the Jamaicans remaining are skilled laborers, working as carpenters or drillers or machine repairmen. Unless they have a specialized skill, these workers earn ten cents per hour, or one dollar each day (since we all work a ten-hour day, six days a week). This may seem like a small amount to be paid for their labor (I know you have earned three times this much in a day with the tips you get), but consider that if they remained at their homes, they would only earn ten cents per day. This means they are making ten times as much in the Zone as they were back home!

Perhaps that is why we observe the celebrations at the docks whenever another boat arrives. All arrivals are required to go through a series of examinations. It all sounds so similar to what Papa described of the medical tests administered to the newly arrived immigrants at his work. The main concern here is that none of the potential workers carry a contagious disease like TB, and none have a preexisting heart condition that would prevent them from being productive, or other conditions such as hernias that would render them useless. Turns out most of them fail and are sent back on the boat that carried them here. Only one in five is allowed to remain. And when they pass the examination, boy! The celebration! They wave their hands, they dance, they hoot, they holler! It's like the crowds back home when their team wins the Series!

Still, when we receive payment as we are lined up outside the pay house, I feel something is very wrong. The line in which I receive payment, the Gold Line, is short, and only the white-skinned laborers are in it. The Silver Line is long, and in it are only the dark-skinned laborers from the Caribbean isles. Sure, silver is valuable, and certainly these workers are earning more for themselves and their families than they would back on the island, but these are the men who are risking their lives. They are the ones placing sticks of dynamite in drilled holes and logs, then running for their lives after lighting the fuse, hoping they will not be the next body that becomes pieces of flesh flying through the air. They are the ones who are often crushed under the enormous wheels of the steam shovels or the railroad cars, and their deaths are announced in the *Canal* (our newspaper) with their number alongside their name—almost to emphasize, or remind us, that their lives are not as valuable as the lives of those with lighter skin.

When Roosevelt visited here in '06, I am told that he frequently stopped the Black workers, speaking with them about the conditions, asking how they were being treated and if they had any complaints. If the conditions have improved here after that visit six years ago, I do not know. But if they have, I only shudder to think of what it was like back then! The homes in which these workers live are shameful. Makes the poor homes of our nation look like mansions. They live in converted railway cars, with walls and roofs made from the remnants of dynamite boxes or discarded ironworks or scraps of lumber. And this is to shield from the relentless, endless downpours! In one room lives four or five bachelors. And me? I have often had one room to myself, and at worst, shared with one roommate.

Yet, few of the workers appear to be bitter. They share the same enthusiasm as most of the workers, the goal of seeing the cut complete, of finishing all the locks, of laying the concrete at Gatun, of one day seeing the water flow from the Atlantic side to the Pacific. Some say it's a shining example of socialism, of how effective and efficient life can be when orchestrated by a fine-tuned government agency. We will be the ambassadors of this fine example upon our return to the States. But as for me, I believe the progress made down here is a combination of many factors, and to attribute any successes to only one factor is fallacious and silly.

By the time you receive this letter, you will all be in the midst of another Series. I want an in-depth analysis, but not of the entire Series and certainly not of each game. We get copies of the papers down here, so I can read those already. What I want is your firsthand analysis, your perceptions. Down here, we workers have a type of scorecard reported weekly in the *Canal*. In it are updated reports of the progress being made on both sides of the cut, the Bas Obispo team digging southwest vs. the Pedro Miguel team digging northeast. The updates are followed with enthusiasm, each of us turning the pages of the weekly paper past all the other headlines to see where our team stands, just as you all rush to page eight or nine to see how the Giants, Highlanders, or Robins performed yesterday. So, Mr. Jennings, from your perch on the steps of the Giants dugout, I want a report on how the team on the northeast shore of our nation is progressing (or subordinating) to the team from the mid-Atlantic shore of the country.

Viva beisbol!

Eli

Postmark: Boston, MA

October 17, 1912

Dear Eli,

This was a doozy! I've been to every game, seen every inning of all the championship games, and this was something special. You have read in the papers and learned of the outcome, but at your request, I will give you some of my insights.

Game 1 – Tuesday, October 8 – Polo Grounds:

"I'm not afraid of Wood's fastball." That's what McGraw was telling the reporters. In the opinion of this club's bat boy, he ought to have been afraid.

The Grounds was packed, and Coogan's Bluff was overflowing. I feared fans may spill over the crest, reminiscent of the fateful playoff game against the Cubs back in '08. A large contingent from Boston filled the seats—Brush reserved enough to suit their needs and even allowed their band onto the field, playing that catchy tune with the annoying words. "Tessie" may be beloved in New England, but she ain't welcome down here. There were so many photographers on the field that the game was delayed as the umpires struggled to clear them into the stands. Even the starting pitching situation was chaotic. McGraw had both Matty and the rookie, Jeff Tesreau, warming up in the outfield. I still can't determine if he was intentionally trying to confuse the Red Sox or if he wanted to see the stuff Matty had. I suppose it was likely a little of both.

Little Napoleon decided to start the rookie. There was grumbling in the stands (and it was echoed in my head) when

Tesreau took the mound in the top of the first. He walked Hooper to start the game, then retired the next three batters. Wood's first two pitches to Devore in the bottom of the inning were out of the zone, but then he went to work, striking out Devore and getting Doyle to ground weakly to short. After Snodgrass singled and Murray walked, Merkle popped a fly to short for the final out. Except for the two runs we scored in the third, both Wood and Tesreau were making quick work of the lineups. Boston scored a run in the sixth, but the real action occurred in the seventh: Boston had two on and two out when Hooper hit a hot liner into left center field between Snodgrass and Devore. Snodgrass called off Devore, which was probably a mistake—I think Devore had a better path to make the catch. The ball skipped past both of them to the fence, giving Boston a 3–2 lead. Yerkes then hit Hooper in from second, Boston was up by two, and Woods was growing stronger as the game progressed. It looked hopeless as he retired the side easily in the eighth.

Murray led the ninth by flying to right for the first out. Then Merkle singled. Buck Herzog singled, moving Merkle to third. Meyers singled cleanly to right, scoring Merkle and advancing the tying run to third. Wood's next three pitches to Fletcher were strikes, all of which our diminutive shortstop swung at and missed. Crandall was due up, and we were out of pinch hitters, or at least pinch hitters that McGraw could rely on. Crandall had come in to pitch in the eighth (Tesreau lost the magic on his curve after that long double by Hooper). Since Crandall is our best-hitting pitcher, there was no reason to pinch-hit, and our best bat off the bench (McCormick) had flied to left in the seventh when he hit for Tesreau. So McGraw let Crandall hit, and Crandall struck out to end the game.

Despite the loss, the way the team fought Woods in the bottom of the ninth was encouraging. And Little Nap told the team as much in the clubhouse and on the northbound train to Boston.

Game 2 – Wednesday, October 9 – Fenway Park:

Matty was horrible—in the first. Hooper led off with a single, Yerkes reached safely when Fletcher muffed a grounder, Speaker bunted for a base hit, and Duffy Lewis hit a sharp grounder to Buck Herzog at third, who made a great throw to the plate, giving us hope that Matty could emerge from this mess. Gardner grounded to second, scoring Yerkes from third. Then Stahl laced a double, scoring two and giving Boston a 3–0 lead. Matty gave up a hit in the second, none in the third, none in the fourth, one in the fifth, none in the sixth, none in the seventh. Going into the eighth, we were down 4–2. We exploded for three runs off Collins, taking the lead, but Boston fought back in their half of the eighth, scoring one more run off Matty and tying the score. Nobody scored in the ninth. Merkle led off the tenth with a triple and scored on McCormick's sacrifice fly. With one out in the bottom of the tenth, Speaker hit a triple off Matty and scored on Duffy Lewis's double. In the eleventh we got two men on, but both were thrown out trying to steal. Matty made quick work of the Sox, retiring them in order. Then the home plate umpire, O'Loughlin, raised his arms in a sweeping gesture, ordering the players off the field on account of darkness. The game would be replayed tomorrow.

Game 3 (replay of Game 2) – Thursday, October 10 – Fenway Park:

Fenway is a new park, and based on what I saw during game two, it appeared all the seats were filled and as many standing fans as they could fit in the outfield had been allowed to enter, but today the crowd was even larger. There were occasional showers throughout the day and even during the game, so we feared this second game would be delayed. But fortunately, we prevailed, outscoring Boston 2–1 and tying the Series at one game. Marquad started and was brilliant, scattering seven hits, allowing only one run in the bottom of the ninth.

Game 4 – Friday, October 11 – Polo Grounds:

It was Wood against Tesreau again. Although we lost, 3–1, I could tell the hitters had figured something out. In particular, they were waiting for Wood's curve, letting the fast ones pass, getting clean singles off the curve. The hope is that we can continue the curve-smacking the next time Wood takes the bump.

Game 5 – Saturday, October 12 – Fenway Park:

Matty was sharp, but Bedient was sharper. I hadn't seen Matty's curve bite so crisply, ever. Maybe it used to bite like this before I joined the team. I hadn't heard Matty's fastball pop Meyers's mitt like it did today for at least the past three years. Still, we lost, 2–1, Matty giving up both runs on back-to-back triples by Hooper and Yerkes (and an error by Doyle) in the third. We're down three games to one. We're going down to New York. The team's mood is down.

Game 6 – Monday, October 14 – Polo Grounds:

This game was over after the first inning. The Giants hitters were not waiting out Boston's pitcher, Buck O'Brien. They saw a pitch to their liking, and they swung. Doyle singled, Murray singled, Merkle doubled. Herzog doubled, Meyers singled, Fletcher singled. By the time the inning closed, we were up 5–0. Although

Boston scored twice in the top of the second, Marquad scattered four hits the rest of the game and allowed no more runs. The final was 5–2, and the Series was now 3–2.

A small ceremony was held after the game—a coin toss—to determine the location of a deciding game, if necessary, since a game was called because of darkness. Boston won the toss. If there was to be a game eight, it would be played at Fenway.

Game 7 – Tuesday, October 15 – Fenway Park:

If game six was over after the first, this game was likely over before it even started.

There was a strange feeling on the field, the same strange feeling that I suppose was in the stands and throughout the country. The "maniac in Milwaukee," the papers called him. A man waiting outside a hotel for Roosevelt to finish a speech walked up to him and shot him in the chest. Isn't it strange enough for our country to have three leading candidates rather than two? Isn't it strange enough for TR to be running outside of the Republican party, against his old buddy, Mr. Taft? And isn't it strange that a man can walk up to our former president and point a gun at his chest? Yet perhaps the strangest thing of it all is that TR is okay. The papers of his speech, folded inside his jacket pocket, apparently padded the impact of the bullet, protecting him from harm!

Were these events dancing in the minds of the players as they warmed up? Were Wood and Tesreau (yes, they were matched up again) distracted as each took the bump? Does this explain why in the top of the first (keep in mind we had scored only four runs in eighteen innings off Wood up to this point) that Devore led the game off with a single, then Doyle hit a single, Snodgrass a double, Merkle a single? Then Meyers a single, Fletcher a single, and Tesreau a single, scoring six runs before the Red Sox came to bat? That Wood was pulled after the first inning? That we clobbered the Sox, 11–4, forcing a decisive eighth game?

And just to add to the strangeness of the day, let me describe to you how we scored our eleventh run in the top of the ninth. Herzog and Wilson (hitting for Meyers) led the inning off with singles, Herzog advancing to third and Wilson taking second. With no outs, Fletch hit a bloop into shallow center, causing Tris Speaker to sprint toward the infield. Wilson, not considering that even the speed of Speaker could catch the bloop, took off for third. Meanwhile, Herzog waited at the third base bag, planning to tag up if Speaker caught up to the fly—which he did, but Speaker was sprinting at such speed, he was in no condition to regain balanced composure to throw the ball to the plate in time to stop Herzog from scoring. Rather, as his momentum carried him toward the infield, he realized that Wilson was still far off the second base bag, so upon regaining his balance, he continued his path toward the infield and stepped on the bag, thus completing an unassisted double play by a center fielder.

Still, this does not complete the strangeness of the day. Prior to the start of the game, while the Royal Rooters were still parading around the perimeter of the field and playing "Tessie" on their horns, the crowd echoing the lyrics, I noticed there were no empty seats anywhere, not even the patch of seats in the left field grandstand that were normally reserved for the Royal Rooters. When the Rooters recognized this minutes later, they began arguing with those who were seated in their usual seats and tried to physically remove them. The commotion caused the police to escort the Rooters behind the right field fence and delayed the game, causing me to wonder if this contributed to Wood's poor outing.

After the game the Rooters took their usual formation on the field, and with the band playing, the leaders shouted through megaphones, chanting the names of Boston's ownership team, after which jeers and boos echoed throughout Fenway. Then even more eeriness settled onto the field as the Royal Rooters, Boston's famed loyalists, began chanting cheers for the Giants.

Despite all the craziness, game eight would be played the next day at Fenway.

Game 8 – Wednesday, October 16 – Fenway Park

Half the stadium was empty. The Rooters rallied the city, convincing many not to attend game eight. Not sure if the Rooters or the 11–4 score the previous day contributed more to the small crowd.

It was the third time in the Series that Matty would pitch against Boston's rookie Hugh Bedient. In game two, the teams tied. In game five, Bedient outdueled Matty, winning 2–1. To me, Matty looked stronger than he did a few days earlier. Again, his pitches were popping Meyers's mitt, and his curves and fadeaways were mystifying Boston hitters. They had four hits and hadn't scored through the first six innings. Meanwhile, we had scored a solitary run in the third and had only five hits. In the seventh, with two out and a man on second, Boston sent up a pinch hitter, Olaf Henriksen, his only plate appearance of the Series (he was used as a pinch runner in game three). Matty's first two pitches were fadeaways, and in hindsight, he should have thrown another. But pitch number three was in Henriksen's groove, and he hit a low liner toward third base. It hit the bag and careened into left field, scoring Stahl and tying the score.

Nobody scored in the eighth.

Nobody scored in the ninth.

With one out in the top of the tenth, Murray smacked a double, followed by a Merkle double. Entering the bottom of the tenth, with Matty on the bump, we had a one-run lead, just three outs from the world championship.

Boston used another pinch hitter, Clyde Engle, who hit a routine fly toward center field. Snodgrass camped under it. The ball popped into his mitt—and the ball popped out of his mitt, falling to the ground. By the time Fred gathered the ball and threw it back to the infield, Engle was standing at second.

I described the game seven atmosphere at Fenway as strange. Now there was a stunned hush, followed by a roaring cheer, mixed with a growing chorus of laughter. I suppose my mouth was aghast, wide open in disbelief. Snodgrass turned and walked back to his position in center, shaking his head. Matty was swinging his glove, swiping the side of his leg, looking out toward Snodgrass in wonder, as if he wasn't sure how to process what had just transpired. The next pitch to Hooper was hit so cleanly and with such strength that the ball jumped from the bat and raced high and deep into center, far over Snodgrass's reach. Nonetheless, with what appeared to me as reckless and hopeless abandon, Fred turned and with his back toward homeplate, raced toward the deepest part of Fenway, with such intent that it seemed he could not possibly track the ball's path. Still, he raced, sprinting, turning his head, raising his arm, and corralling the ball in his glove—then, turning, he threw the ball back to Murray, preventing Engle from advancing to third.

What I had just witnessed was more than the greatest catch or the most crucial piece of defensive genius in a World Series game. It was someone who desperately needed an opportunity to prove his worth, and he did.

Matty walked Yerkes, I think intentionally, to hopefully set up a game-ending double play.

Speaker was up next. He hit .383 during the season and during the eight games showed off the talent that one would expect. On Matty's first pitch he hit a flare pop fly into foul territory, just to the left of the first base bag. Merkle stepped to his left, camping under it. Matty jogged toward the foul line, halfway between home and first, and Meyers tossed his mask and raced forward toward Merkle. I heard the fans jeering and the Boston players shouting, screaming with all their strength, "Matty! Matty!" This affected Merkle, it seemed, to back away from the path of the ball's descent. I saw all three of our players stop in their tracks, then watch the ball fall between the three of them in foul territory.

I saw them argue. Even Matty, who *always* kept his cool and never showed anger at a teammate's miscue, was clearly miffed at both Merkle and Meyers.

"You will pay for that, Matty," I heard Speaker shout as he stepped back into the box.

On the next pitch, Mr. Speaker lined a single, scoring Engle and sending Yerkes to third. The score was tied, and there was only one out. Speaker had advanced to second on the throw to the plate, so Matty intentionally walked Duffy Lewis, loading the bases. Larry Gardner hit a deep fly into right field. After catching the ball, Josh Devore threw it back toward the plate with all his strength, but it hadn't even reached the mound by the time Yerkes had crossed home, scoring the winning run of the game and the Series.

If Fenway had been filled to capacity as it was in all the other games, I can only imagine the celebration that would have resulted when the winning run scored. However, no such celebratory craziness erupted. Sure, there was applause, and sure, there were fans shouting, but seventeen thousand fans are not as boisterous as thirty-five thousand. Whereas the field would have been swarming with adoring fans, what I saw was some isolated young men, not much older than me, jumping onto the field, patting Speaker and Hooper and Wood on the back.

Matty had walked back to the dugout, set his glove on the bench, and placed his hands over his eyes. When he looked up, I saw the redness, the tears.

I saw him in '05. He made it look so easy. The A's got even with him last year. This year the Sox defeated him. Sure, he wasn't the Matty of yesterday, pitching twenty-seven innings of shutout ball, but he was still brilliant, still Matty. And yet he didn't even win one game. When I saw him weeping like a kid, he was still my hero, still dignified, still kind, still Matty.

If I don't write again before the holidays, hope you have a merry Christmas and happy Chanukah.

William

1913

——∞——

Postmark: Canal Zone

January 13, 1913

William,

The weather here changes without warning—dark skies, pouring rain, and minutes later, clear skies and sunshine. Each day when those clouds drift into the horizon and are replaced by blue above and all around, I breathe in deeply, close my eyes, smile, and silently thank Master of universe. You see, this routine of weather in the Zone, the clouds being replaced by the intensity of blue, resonates inside me as I think of the last three months.

Just after I received your last letter detailing the Series, I fell ill. In fact, the day I received your letter, I was so weak and nauseous that I hadn't the strength to open the envelope, let alone attempt to read and make sense of what you had written. My only desire that day and most of the days that followed was for life to end. This desire increased exponentially as the days passed into November.

The best way I can describe my experience is to echo the words of the man who wrote the following lines.

You are going to have the fever,
Yellow eyes!
In about ten days from now
Iron bands will clamp your brow
Your tongue will resemble curdled cream
A rusty streak the center seam
Your mouth will taste of untold things
With claws and horns and insects and wings
Your head will weigh a ton or more,
And forty gales within it roar!

The days in the infirmary were filled with nightmares. They were one long nightmare. My one enduring hope was to sleep so I may escape the torment of the symptoms, only to enter the torment awaiting me in my dreams. My greatest comfort was weeping, begging Master of the universe to let my life end. I found this helped me have a more pleasant rest. But I woke, seeing the deteriorating condition of my roommates, smelling the stinging smell of alcohol around me, looking at my skin and the beads of sweat dropping onto the drenched bed sheets. I felt my parched throat and my pounding headache, sharp and pulling pain in my back and legs, a restlessness to jump from my body, in hope of escaping all the miserable sensations I was experiencing. I saw blotches of blackened blood on the bedsheets around my chest, reminding me of the endless coughing fits followed by the vomiting of blood, the sudden drops in my temperature, the shivering, the fever.

Then on the morning of November 9, I awoke—no sweating, no headache, mind clear. I looked outside the window near my bed. A cloud was moving quickly across the sky, from my vantage point moving from the left pane to the right pane. Within seconds it was out of sight, replaced by the blue Panamanian sky. I had never felt such gratitude and relief and joy. I had an appetite! I had more strength! I had desire! I was alive!

The doctors and nurses tell me that my symptoms, pain, and discomfort were quite minor compared to what other yellow fever victims endure. Many had died. I, however, have survived to write this letter. I was still weak and my mind clouded, so writing a letter, even reading and understanding your letter, was challenging. Thus, the two-month delay.

I enjoyed your rendering of the Series. I felt the pain as you described Snod's dropped fly and the untouched foul by Speaker. Papa once told me that I would likely never match the catalog of suffering endured by Job, but that does not mean I would never suffer. "In fact," I remember him saying, "the message of Job is that suffering is a fact of life. We, like Job's friends, may try to explain the cause of suffering, the things we have done to warrant the onslaught of pain, or the way we ought to live in order to minimize the chances of catastrophic events. There may be elements of truth in any of these lines of thought, but," he told me, "suffer you will. Job teaches us *how* to suffer, not how to avoid suffering."

Success in '05 was wonderful. Matty was raised from a great pitcher to a national hero, and McGraw was riding high. The loss this year to the Sox and last year to Mack's Athletics has humbled our Giants. It is definitely not suffering in the classic sense, but I am curious as to how you all will respond. Will Little Napoleon and his generals rise from two consecutive defeats and emerge from the ashes to win the Series in 1913?

What is happening here is a manifestation of my father's teachings. All the suffering and failures experienced by the French effort thirty years ago, all the deaths and illnesses we have endured over the past ten years—could we have expected anything less?

It was the genius of Dr. Gorgas that helped us eradicate malaria in the Zone. It was the genius of all the engineers that came up with the lock concept for the canal. It was the wonderful management of John Stevens and General Goethals that has led us to the verge of completion. But none of this would have amounted to much without the willingness of all the workers to endure the humidity, the illness, the death, the suffering. As Papa said, "Suffer you will."

The consensus of the French was to dig a canal though the narrowest region of Panama. Though they failed, our effort began on this same premise. It was not until our digging began, as late as 1906, that the lock option created a debate. One of the early proponents for a lock was the French engineer Philippe Bunau-Varilla. If it weren't for Stevens and others convincing Roosevelt of the useless efforts in digging a sea-level canal (mainly because of endless landslides), the tide may not have turned. By early '07 the Senate changed its stance and approved the lock option.

Here I stand at the bottom of a man-made lake. Lake Gatun, once a large expanse of forest, is now stripped of trees, many of which were blown to pieces by countless sticks of dynamite. What used to be acres of fertile soil is now laid with concrete. I look to my left and right, and I feel as small and insignificant as an ant. Extending in both directions are towers of concrete, gray faceless structures taller than the buildings in Manhattan. In a few months the two digging crews will finally meet, completing the Culebra Cut. Where I now sit, eat my lunch, and write this letter, this very spot will be submerged under forty or fifty feet of water. The power from this stored energy will control the locks, enabling the ships to rise and fall, to move from Pacific to Atlantic, from Atlantic to Pacific.

If the schedule is not interrupted by slides (now minimal), festivities to celebrate its opening are planned for the fall, and full operation will begin when you are in the midst of your freshman studies at whichever college you decide to attend.

Tu amigo,

Eli

Postmark: New York, NY

April 2, 1913

Dear Eli,

I am deeply sad about your being sick. And I am very happy that you are better. The things you suffered, the things you write about suffering, have bothered me as early as my days at St. Mary's. I don't ask the *why* because I don't think it is something that can be answered. Why ought I to waste time on trying to figure something out that can't be figured out? Seems my energy would be better spent trying to figure out how to survive or emerge if something bad happens. My job is to get up and sell the papers. Your job is to help with the canal. Matty, McGraw, and the rest of the team, they must find a way to resume their winning play as the new season begins.

What angers me, what has gotten a fire burning inside, is the things people do to other people that cause this suffering. For almost a year now I have been attending the public school with Naomi, Mara, and David—walking David to his school, then walking across the street with the twins to our high school. When my last class is let out, the three of them are sitting on a bench, waiting for me to walk them to their classes at temple. More than once, the girls' eyes have been red and they were sniffling. The first day this happened, David pointed to his face, shifting his eyes toward Mara, letting me know that the tears resulted from something to do with the red mark underneath her right eye. Mara was looking at the ground, examining in detail, it seemed, the intricacies of the leaves' location on the dirt beneath the bench. She held her hand just above the mark, not quite scratching it, just hovering above it, as if caressing it may help erase it. Naomi said softly, "They tease, tease, tease, as if she can't hear them. They break red crayons and rub them on their faces or use paint from art class and rub it under their eyes. 'Look,' they say to one another, 'you know my twin sister?' and they giggle, giggle, giggle . . ."

And these are high schoolers?

And it gets worse. I've wondered why they are always alone on the bench, such friendly kids, why have I never met any of their friends from their classes. David's friends have vanished. I began noticing the looks kids give them as they walk by the bench. And the parents! They wrap their arms around their kids as they pick them up in front of the school, escorting them, maneuvering as they walk past the bench on which the twins and David wait, as if to protect their children from your three younger siblings. And then I see the same look on the faces of the parents as I saw on the faces of their children.

"You have your own schools," one young boy said the other day. "You don't belong here."

"Why put them through this?" a parent said to me this afternoon. "Your kind are not welcome here."

So, Eli, how long has this been happening? Didn't you go to this same school? The kids seem sad, but not angry or enraged like I feel they should be. Within a couple minutes after we leave the bench, the girls are chatting or humming tunes, and David is punching my arm, trying to start a friendly boxing match. As we enter the temple classroom, the other kids look over their shoulders at your siblings, and the expressions on these faces are identical to the expressions we saw from the kids at the public school. How is this possible?

I would like to punch each of those smug-looking kids that walk past your brother and sisters on the bench. I'd like to chase them across the street with hopes that an automobile crosses their path and squishes them under its tires. I'd like to pick up each of those kids at temple, hold them in the air, brace them against the wall, and shake them until they acknowledge that David, Naomi, and Mara are to be treated with every ounce of kindness they deserve.

Add to this the ribbing Meyers receives on a daily basis from the visiting team and their fans. I've always been bothered by the hooting that echoes after Meyers—fans thinking they are ingenious for mocking his Indian heritage. There are rumors that the Giants may be seeking to sign the Olympic hero for next season. How, I wonder, would a fan have the nerve to taunt Mr. Thorpe? I am curious to see how he would be received.

My blood boils as I sit on the dugout steps, hearing all the whooping calls. As much as I'd like to teach the classmates of the kids a lesson, I'd like to jump into the stands and teach those low-class baseball fans a lesson! I guess it's a good thing I haven't done any of this. If I had, my acceptance to Harvard would likely have been denied. Yes, you read it correctly! I am going to Harvard!

I am shocked, I am excited, and I am scared. My acceptance would not have been possible without the two letters written on my behalf. When McGraw learned of my intention, he insisted on writing to the president of the college. Though I have no idea what the letter included, I am sure it was free of the expletives I regularly hear from him. The second letter was obtained by Uncle Nathan. I still shake with utter inexpressible gratitude to him. About six months ago he tracked down TR—I think he addressed the letter to his home in Sagamore Hill. Within a month he received a response, an envelope sealed with Roosevelt's presidential seal, and included was a copy of the letter he had written. All that he wrote, all that I read, could have come from one source only: Uncle Nathan. My gratitude and surprise results from the mixture that a former president would take the time to write a recommendation letter to his alma mater for someone he had never met, that your uncle thinks highly enough of me to convince someone of TR's prominence of my qualities, and that TR trusts Uncle Nathan's estimation of my character. Nothing I could have ever dreamed! Within seven months, if I survive and conquer the battery of entrance exams, I will be residing in Cambridge!

Your friend,

William

Postmark: Canal Zone

May 21, 1913

William,

Yes, I am aware of what the kids endure. Although Ruth and I both faced the same unwelcome looks at the public school, we were spared the unfriendliness at temple. Papa was respected and revered. Many of our neighbors had benefited from his position at the immigration station. Families had been reunited because of his influence and mediation. As a result, the parents of our classmates would not tolerate disrespect for the family of Officer Chalmers. Now that Papa has been gone for five years, most of this goodwill has vanished. Naomi, Mara, and David are left with no option but to endure the ugly stares, unwelcome gestures, and nasty words.

Our freedom in America is priceless. It includes our freedom that all men have, regardless of a constitution that protects their legal rights, the liberty to react to *bad* in ways that are *good*. Papa and Mama sat me down the day I hit a boy after he chanted on the playground, teasing me. "Sheeny, sheeny, sheeny," he said, pointing at me, laughing, throwing dirt, and spitting. "Ain't this what you sheenies did to Jesus?" he shouted.

"No matter what others do," Papa told me, "even if they do it in his name, you must do as he teaches. That, son, is the choice you have. You will always have this choice. Nobody can take this choice from you."

As you have seen in the ways the twins and David have handled the situation, they also have received these words of encouragement from Papa, Mama, Ruthie, and me. It is a blessing for me to hear of their faithful obedience.

Congratulations on your acceptance to Harvard! I am excited for you and confident that you will excel in your studies. Do you have an inkling of the field of study you will pursue?

Now for an update from the Canal Zone. On Tuesday, May 20, shovel 222 met shovel 230. It was all we could talk about. Shouts of celebration began as the two shovels met, and like a telegraph wire, the shouting resounded eastward and westward—toward Empire, toward Pedro Miguel. For over seven years shovels and crews had been tirelessly digging, blowing, excavating. Now the cut was complete, and soon water will be running freely between the oceans. Soon, ships will be passing through.

Should be coming home shortly.

See you soon,

Eli

Postmark: Boston, MA

September 18, 1913

Dear Eli,

I envy you, what you have done, what you have seen and accomplished. All the wonder we felt staring at the Williamsburg Bridge pales in contrast to all you have accomplished in Panama.

I had always wanted to thank the men who built the bridges of our city, constructed the elevated trains, dug the tunnels for the subways, but I never knew who those men might be. Was it someone to whom I sold a paper this morning? Was it the man who caught a foul ball at the Grounds this afternoon? Was it one of those who rest underneath the headstones I pass each day?

But you I know!

You I can thank!

You I can revere!

Classes started a couple weeks ago. My freshman European history class began with detailed study of the Napoleonic Wars. Needless to say, I savored each lecture. Funny thing occurred during the first day of class as our professor was describing Napoleon's Egyptian campaign prior to his ascension to the throne. The image of Napoleon, though I had seen pictures of his face and dark hair and strong nose, transformed into the face of Little Napoleon—Mugsy McGraw. And when I read of Marshal Ney, I envisioned Matty, his Giants uniform cast off in favor of the French military garb. Grouchy became Marquad, and Gneisenau became Meyers.

My days are filled with study and practice. Yes, practice! Several things have developed since I last wrote. As my days with the Giants neared their end in early June, Matty beckoned me to his side as he was tossing warm-ups in the outfield to Meyers and asked if I planned to pitch for the ball club in Cambridge. I shrugged and told him I didn't think I had enough skills to make the team. Matty extended his right arm and invited me to stand beside him. "Look," he said, as he gripped the ball, engulfing it in the palm of his hand. "When you release it, twist your arm inward, twisting your hand as you release the ball toward the plate." As he did it, I caught the closest glimpse of his fadeaway that I had ever seen. Arching toward Meyers, it bit a hard right, shooting down, making it necessary for Meyers to shuffle and move his mitt to catch the pitch.

Meyers tossed the ball back to Matty.

"You try it," he said, handing me the ball.

He stepped back, held my hand, and guided my fingers on the correct location of the seams.

My first attempt was poor. It hit the dirt several feet in front of Meyers.

Ten minutes later my pitch had a subtle arc. Within a week, it was a "bite"—not as sharp and defined as Matty's, but a bewildering pitch for those who had never seen it. By the time I arrived in Cambridge, it was breaking almost as deceptively as Matty's.

This, in combination with McGraw lobbying Coach Mitchell on my behalf, created an opportunity for me to try out. Which brings me to the other major development.

I received a letter from Merlin in early August, informing me that he also had been accepted at Harvard. Merlin is smart. I know that. But I hadn't realized he was as smart as he is, graduating at the top of his class. But more than this, he held the highest batting average of all high school seniors in the state of Illinois, earning him a baseball scholarship and the promise of a starting position in the outfield.

So, after my successful tryout, Merlin and I are teammates. We are also roommates!

Though I am busy, I keep tabs on the Giants' progress. Since late June they have not relinquished first place, and it appears they will be facing Mack's Athletics again. Come early October, I will miss my first World Series game.

I have benefited much from you, your father, your mother, Uncle Nathan, McGraw, and now Matty. None of this would be possible without the efforts and kindness I received from you all. As I look back on my years with the Giants, I have mixed reactions. Sure, I have lived a dream that most boys would never think possible, but I have also seen up close the heartache of losing: the debacle in '08, then the consecutive losses in '11 and '12. Even McGraw, with all his bad traits, deserves better! And Matty. Isn't there some way I could honor him? Some way I could show how much worth he brings to this team, to our city, to me?

See you soon?

William

Postmark: Canal Zone

October 6, 1913

William,

Ten days ago we saw our dreams fulfilled. Around 11:00 a.m. on Friday morning, September 26, the *Gatun,* a small tugboat named after the lake, entered the upper locks. Around 5:00 p.m. it entered the lower locks. Just before 7:00 p.m. it entered Lake Gatun—the first successful voyage through the canal!

I suspect I will be leaving soon and hope to journey to New England, visit you and Merlin, and watch one of your early games next spring.

With regard to your desire to pay homage to Mr. Mathewson, I suspect that your particular gift of reporting players' strengths and weaknesses could be utilized. May I suggest that you create a special T-report in which your honor for Matty could best be displayed.

Your amigo,

Eli

Postmark: Boston, MA

October 11, 1913

Dear Eli,

Here it is, my homage to Matty, just as you suggested.

After missing the first four games (the first four championship games I have ever missed), I caught a train from Boston on Saturday morning, arriving just in time to watch the events unfold from my perch atop Coogan's Bluff. At this point, the Athletics were holding a 3–1 lead in the Series.

How the Mighty Have Fallen

Your glory, O Harlem, lies slain on the field of the Grounds!
How the mighty have fallen!
Tell it not in the Windy City,
Proclaim it not in Steel City's streets—
Or the fans of the Cubs will rejoice,
The Pirates' bugs exult.

You bluff of Coogan,
Let there be no triumph or applauds,
No raucous cheering.
For there the warrior of our team was defiled!
The arm of Matty, anointed with victory no more.

From the splendid swing of Honus,
From the heavy wood of Baker,
The fadeaway of Matty did not turn back,
Nor the cunning of his wit return empty.

Christopher Mathewson, beloved and reliable!
At home and on the road you were feared.
Your straight ones were swifter than eagles,
Your fadeaways baffling all batsmen.

O fans of New York, weep over Big Six—
He clothed the Grounds with victory,
He brought pride and pennants to our city.

How the mighty have fallen
In the midst of the battle!

In '05 he allowed no runs,
Though he pitched three full games,
Adorning our field with a championship flag.
In '01 he won twenty games; in '03 he won thirty.
In '04 it was thirty-three; in '05, thirty-one.
Twenty-two, twenty-four, thirty-seven, twenty-five,
Twenty-seven, twenty-six, twenty-three
From '06 through 1912.

This season he won another twenty-five.
He walked no batsmen from mid-June through mid-July,
Sixty-eight consecutive frames.
Yet, another flag has not flown over our field . . .

In '08 a base-running blunder cost the pennant.
In 1911 there were sign stealings and fat pitches and costly
  errors.
In '12 it was a dropped fly ball, a foul ball that ought to have
  been caught.

And this year, after losing the first battle against Mr. Mack's
  Athletics,
Big Six pitched nine innings of shutout. So did the A's Mr.
  Plank.
In the tenth Matty hit in the game's first run; he scored the
  second.
He completed a ten-inning shutout victory.
Games three and four were filled with poor pitching and
  fielding—and losses.
The team was relying on Matty for game five—but
More costly errors. After eight innings, down 3–1,
Matty retired Mack's team in order. One-two-three to end
  the ninth.
He walked to the dugout . . .
Mugsy signaled for a pinch hitter . . .

Big Six wrapped his mackinaw over his shoulders;
He scurried toward the clubhouse in deep center field. His
*   scurry became a shuffle*
As the mackinaw slipped from his shoulders to the ground,
*   just past second base,*
The bat boy ran from the dugout steps to his side;
He picked up the soldier's fallen overcoat, wrapping it back
*   over the warrior's shoulders.*
Matty placed his hand atop the lad's head, then continued
*   his march,*
Disappearing beyond the center field fence.

How the mighty have fallen,
And the weapon of our Giants is no more!

For Further Reading

Game events described in the narrative are based on the summaries and box scores from accounts appearing in the main editions of the following newspapers:

Chicago Tribune (October 9–13, 1907; September 5, 24, and 28, 1908; October 9–15, 1908; October 21–24, 1910)

Philadelphia Inquirer (April 17, 1908; September 30, 1908; October 3–4, 1908; October 18–19, 1910; October 15 and 17, 1911)

Pittsburgh Post (October 9–17, 1909)

Boston Globe (October 7–17, 1912)

New York Tribune (October 26, 1911)

New York Times (September 23, 2008; October 15–27, 1911; October 9–17, 1912; October 8–12, 1913)

Accounts and perspectives of the events surrounding the 1908 playoff game between the Cubs and Giants can be found in numerous works of baseball history: *Matty: An American Hero* by Ray Robinson, *Christy Mathewson, the Christian Gentleman* by Bob Gaines, *Pitching in a Pinch* by Christy Mathewson, *My Thirty Years in Baseball* by John McGraw, *The Old Ball Game* by Frank Deford, and the firsthand accounts of Fred Snodgrass, Al Birdwell, and Hans Lobert in *The Glory of Their Times*.

The travails and successes in the career of Harry Coveleski are mentioned in the biographies by Gaines and Robinson, the firsthand account of Fred Snodgrass, and the autobiographies by Mathewson and McGraw.

Luther Taylor's legacy is described in detail by Darryl Brock in *Havana Heat*. Further discussion of Taylor and his contributions to the Giants' success as well as his sense of humor and on-the-field antics can be found in McGraw's autobiography and Frank Deford's *The Old Ball Game*.

The Giants mascot, Charley Faust, makes regular appearances in many of the works listed above.

Accounts of the fire at the Triangle Shirt Factory can be read in the Sunday edition of the *New York Times*, March 26, 1911. The Polo Grounds fire and the impacts it had on the Giants' season are described in most of the books previously listed.

Insights into the lives of bat boys during various eras of baseball history are portrayed in *Innocence and Wonder* by Neil Isaacs.

The difficulties and prejudices experienced by Jewish believers in the late nineteenth and early twentieth centuries are described by Leopold Cohn in *To an Ancient People*.

The poem "Yellow Eyes" was written by James Stanley Gilbert.

Finally, for a thorough, insightful, and enjoyably long read of the construction and completion of the Panama Canal, read David McCullough's *The Path Between the Seas*.

Acknowledgments

The editing and proofing skills of Karen Cleghorn have helped create a story that flows. I am sincerely appreciative for the time and effort she invests in making the narrative much more than it was before it met her eyes. In addition, I would like to thank Sally Hanan and her team at Inksnatcher for assisting with typesetting and cover design.

I am indebted to the sportswriters who compiled the box scores and wrote game summaries following each game of the World Series between 1907 and 1913. In addition, I am grateful to many of their colleagues who worked in other departments of our nation's leading newspapers. Often, the narrative evolved in directions I had not anticipated based on the events described on pages outside of the sports section.

I would also like to thank the National Baseball Hall of Fame and Museum in Cooperstown, New York, for authorizing the use of Mugsy and Matty's photograph for the front cover.